SWAMP NYMPH

SWAMP NYMPH

JOHN BURTON THOMPSON

CUTTING EDGE

ISBN-13: 978-1-952138-27-0

Published by
Cutting Edge Publishing
PO Box 8212
Calabasas, CA 91372
www.cuttingedgebooks.com

CHAPTER ONE

Charles Corbett Carraway, the Third, did not feel well. In fact, he felt so poorly that he was seriously considering doing himself mortal injury. He drove his black Thunderbird up to the front of the big, three-storied house, got out and slipped the gear into neutral. The car, freed of engine drag, drifted down the inclined driveway and crashed into a solid bank of carefully cultivated lagustrums that guarded the curve where the driveway turned back toward the street. Peculiarly, he felt a sense of sadistic revenge. Not against the car which he liked immensely, but the gesture... "I'll show'em," he said aloud. He flushed in the darkness. That was a childish thing to do... smashing good shrubbery... scarring the car most likely, then reacting that he had *showed* someone something. He felt an apprehensive chill. Was he losing his grip? Was he deteriorating mentally?

He walked up the broad stone steps and was winded when he reached the top. Thirty years old, he said to himself, and I can't climb a short flight of steps without gasping for breath. His mind dropped back a few years as he sat on a porch chair to recover. Korea... he had been a fighting man, as hard as nails and twice as tough. He had had steel in his guts and iron in his blood. He felt the soft expanse of his stomach and grimaced as he dug up a fist full of blubber. The back of his neck ached fiercely... tension headache the doctor called it. His belly ached like a sore tooth. Nervous stomach the doctor had called-it and gave him tiny white pills to take that made his throat and mouth dry. They gave only temporary relief. Then the psychiatrist, the Freudian fool... He

1

made a face. Deserved it ... for going in the first place His trouble was not the mystery of cause but what to do about it. After all, he had been more or less promised to Lavender Masefield for years. Marrying her was a mistake from the first but even with a new and soaring sense *of* war-spawned self-confidence, he had cleaved to the line and married her fifteen months after he was discharged.

Lavender had been a soft, white, rose and ebony courtesan for the first three months, a matter that gathered significance as time passed. Charles Corbett Carraway, the Third, had considered himself a fairly well informed modem man, the master of his own bed if not a rollicking love pirate. Lavender, from the first, seemed to instinctively know her way with more surety and it was certain that her inventiveness surpassed his own by too much to mention. He never mentioned it. Indeed, did not even think of it for a long time. Then came the question, how did a virgin become so educated? The answer was not long coming after his newness had worn off and as a playfellow he'd begun to pall. Lavender gave evidence of this in numerous ways ... becoming pettish and longing for newness ... anything to give marriage a different flavor. As far as Charles was concerned there was a limit to what degree newness and versatility could be maintained in spite of the fact that she had conceived of some rare departures from the ancient game.

She blamed him at first, later became annoyed and later still, incensed. Then inexplicably she began to cool. This was a shock, coming as it had on the heels of her performance that had at first amazed, then delighted him.

Lavender was from one of the first families in the big industrial city as was Charles Corbett Carraway, the Third, and that she had ever strayed from the path was to him, unthinkable. That is, he once thought so. Now he knew differently and so far from holding her to the paths of loyalty, her position became a refuge from which she dared greatly, eagerly, consistently and with little thought as to the consequences. Their associates were all either executives and their wives and families, department heads, family scions, or others equally high in the economic-social strata.

Carraway Chemicals, an old, respected and flourishing firm, had many highly paid executives, scientists and experts of various sorts who, enjoying the genial Carraway hospitality, were in and out of the solid old mansion, socially, more often than they were on business matters, something started by Charles Corbett Carraway the First, as a means of insuring easy association and free discussion between management and production. A man who had broken your bread and drunk your wine was not likely to feel insecure and backward in discussing matters that might at first glance seem discommoding to the higher echelons.

The older Carraways had realized that if the rifts down the line from top management were too great, those at the top were almost incommunicado, and when at last the news did reach them, damage had inevitably been done. They strove to keep Carraway Chemicals on the big-happy-family basis and succeeded to whatever degree such things ever succeed. As a result, the house was always full of people, eating, drinking, playing golf on the company course, riding around the estate on the finest horseflesh that could be had or playing tennis on the best courts that could be constructed.

As a further result, Charles, one afternoon, after a hard day at work, arrived home early and found Lavender in a state that could hardly come under the genteel term compromising, since it is a term that suggests light, if potentially dangerous, dalliance. Dr. Frank Floyd and Lavender were not dallying by the most charitable stretch of the imagination. They had been playing tennis ... or so it might seem, and had gone to the little shower house that served both the courts and the swimming pool. Apparently they had intended to top off several hard sets of tennis with a dip in the pool and had progressed only to the stage where they were ready for a highly private swim.

Wandering about the grounds absently, wondering where his wife was, Charles heard a single sharp utterance that he had heard before on other occasions but never in the shower house. Closer examination revealed what he suspected had happened and Lavender, streaked with sweat and ripped with passion, looked directly into his prying eyes. He looked back, watching the spasm of her long fine muscles, the exorbitant response of her body and the passion-blasted face that went through tortured grimaces, muffling vocal outcry with the greatest effort. Then he realized that she had looked at him but hadn't seen him and the awakening was a rude one.

Dr. Floyd, also intent on the game, had not seen him, so Charles faded into the shrubbery and went to his room. He missed dinner that night and not a soul missed him enough to wonder what his trouble was but Edna, the appallingly attractive Swedish maid who cherished a secret admiration for her master. She had come to the room, knocked discreetly, and entered at his invitation.

"Is anything wrong, sir? You didn't come to dinner."

He looked up stupidly. "Wrong? Er ... no ... Not feeling up to snuff."

"Mr. Carraway ..." She stopped, wondering if she might invite a confidence. What he now knew she had long known for the simple reason that human frailty was not a matter for amazement or surprise to Edna. Edna had been reared on a large farm in Nebraska and the only reason why she was not there instead of a maid in a rich man's house was that she wanted to see how the other half lived ... for at least a few years before she went back to Nebraska and married Sven, Arid, Karl, or Ole.

Edna knew a great deal more of life on both sides of its face than many a girl twice her age. She had discovered early where and how off-springs were produced and that the difference between the way it was achieved between the human and the animal was not in the essentials but in such less important matters as taste, regard for spectators, and a certain human preference for the night hours.

"What, Edna?"

Edna's great china-blue eyes misted over. "You're unhappy and I think I know why."

From that moment on Edna ceased being a mere servant and became a person, an exceedingly lovely person. Charles Corbett Carraway, the Third, raised his head slowly and looked at her. She stood proudly and her uniform, while just another uniform, could not begin to defile the outline of the extravagant body that wore it. From her chin to her feet she was a symphony of billowing curves, big... she was not a small girl, but so deftly turned, so obviously high in quality, so tenderly finished in the smallest detail that his mouth suddenly went dry as though he had taken an overdose of his stomach pills. Her skin was fair and so appallingly smooth that he began to wonder why he had never really looked at this marvelous creature before. She stirred beneath his frank gaze and he woke to reality.

"Sorry," he muttered. "Sorry... Why do you concern yourself about me?"

"You missed dinner," she said, with such heart-aching gentleness that his chest began to feel tight and smothery. "You've been unhappy. I've seen it. I don't think you've done anything to deserve it. I like you. You've always been polite and nice to me... even if I am just a part of the general scene..." She stopped. She would be saying too much if she didn't call a halt.

"Thanks," he said huskily. "It seems that you're about the only one around this draughty museum who ever thinks about me."

"Yes, I know. I've seen her. I saw you wandering this afternoon. I saw you come in and I knew you'd..."

He chuckled despairingly as though to prevent some less pleasing sound from issuing. "Yes... I saw them... her. Dr. Floyd is a very valuable man to the company. He developed our new plastic, Carranyl."

Suddenly, for the first time in too long to remember, Charles Carraway wanted his mother. He wanted her with such an aching sincerity that he drew up in pain and grasped his face with his hands. He had had several drinks and his emotional threshold was low. Scalding tears poured through his taut fingers and his body writhed with an effort to keep it from humping and shaking like a child sobbing. With a soft sound of pity, Edna dropped to her knees before him and forcing his hands away from his face, took his head in her arms and held it close to her breast. Tears filled her big eyes and coursed down her cheeks unnoticed. For a long time she held him until the storm subsided and he became rational again. He stood up and took a shuddering sigh.

"What a wonderful person ... you are," he said unsteadily.

She remained on her knees before him and looked up into his eyes.

"Am I? Because I have a little human kindness and like you? Because I think you're a fine man? Is it because of that?"

"No," he said, "I think it's because of something inexpressibly fine about you ... as a person. I know now because you've just shown me what you're really like, but you were that way before you stepped into the room."

All of a sudden an overpowering affection for this simple, wonderful girl overcame him, he knelt and they faced each other on their knees.

"This is poor payment for your kindness because in a way it asks for more kindness, but I'd like to kiss you."

Her eyes didn't waver, and the smile was so achingly sweet that Charles felt like crying again.

"I'd like that," she said gently. "In fact, I've wondered how it would be to kiss you." She swayed forward into his arms, their lips met and melted into each other. For a long moment Charles felt that he had been caught in the leaping arc of two heavy voltage lines.

The impact shocked him to such an extent that he felt himself holding her for support and never had he felt solider support. She was soft and feminine but Edna Ivorsen had been reared to labor and beneath her soft exterior were muscles. She could feel the uncertainty of his mind, the ache and longing, the hurt and disappointments that had plagued him ever since childhood when he began to know that he was being groomed for the leadership of a great organization. He had subconsciously resented and resisted ever since but he had never admitted it even to himself. He was a nonconformist who had forced himself to conform and now it was beginning to tell. Through the lips of this wonderful woman everything seemed to break loose. It was some time later before they parted and both realized it had been a new experience for them.

Edna was warmly uplifted because she knew what a purging he had undergone. With flawless feminine intuition she knew he needed more ... she doubted that he knew it, even though she fitted him warmly from knee to breast and not once had she withdrawn any of herself. Being wiser and therefore unafraid of such things, she knew that he would feel the same thing she had felt first, a thick sickening sweet throb that seemed to swell within her stimulated by his closeness, triggered by the fact that she was all woman, sensitive to the pressure of his body, the heat she was absorbing and the heat she knew she was radiating.

With a little shiver she clutched him closer ... then she *knew* what he felt because at that precise moment he gave evidence that he could not deny. Suddenly she felt a boneless dizziness attacking her and she swayed a little, her head falling forward and her lips meeting his again, wet, hot, open for the darting weapons to engage and frighten them with the sweet combat.

To him came belated, but strong, a kind of super-consciousness, an acute awareness of her closeness followed closely by a wave of chilling embarrassment that his physical self had preceded his conscious reaction ... and she knew. She couldn't help knowing. Like a glove she fitted him and his skin drank in the lifegiving warmth she radiated so liberally.

He was conscious of the spread of her high breasts where they were pressed against him, the warm pressure of the slightly rounded hillock of her stomach, the acquiescence, if not belligerence, of her loins and the hard-soft contours of her thighs pressed against his.

A shudder went over him, a shudder that accentuated their closeness and sent his mouth widening, begging, throbbing in search of deeper contact, searching for release from the need that rode his back like a specter of demand. The unconscious movement against her released her from mere acquiescence and from her own instinct came motion equally as free of volition but with the objectivity of an instinct that is older than woman.

Realizing now for the first time that she was offering more than he had any right to take, he released her lips and looked into her big eyes with something akin to fright.

"Edna … this is terrible …" He gasped and caught her shoulders. He tried to back away but her arms about his waist wouldn't allow it.

"No" It was a whisper that moved her wet kiss-burnished lips in such a delightful smile that he kissed her again and squeezed her with such a burst of affection that she gasped with pain.

"No," she said again when he released her. "What's terrible about it?"

"You don't think so?"

"No."

"Edna, be truthful with me now. Have you ever before?'

"No."

"Then …"

"Listen to me. I come from a pretty big farm. I was reared with boys and men all around me. I know what they think and I've had my chances. I have no moral scruples against enjoying my senses. I had several reasons for avoiding their clumsy charges. First, I knew enough about physiology to realize the danger. Second, I'm afraid my standards were a little above the usual girl's. The men who wanted me were almost invariably smelly ... stale milk and barnyard smells ... gesture baths on Saturday night. I suppose I got this attitude from my mother. She's a little hipped on the subject of personal cleanliness." She caught his hands and examined his fingernails. "See what I mean?"

Charles felt a sudden pride in the fact that his nails were well manicured and clean. So, as a matter of fact, was the rest of him. He, too, was something of a fetishist about personal cleanliness. He grinned at her.

"We would certainly look silly to anyone else ... kneeling here like this ... and my knees are beginning to complain."

They both flushed a little and stood up. "So you see," she continued, "the reasons why. Although I'm not against men, I didn't accept any attempts from those I knew."

They were standing but he was aware that she was still in contact. The warmth of her sumptuous body more noticeable now than before ... and the fit was better.

He shook his head. "It doesn't seem right. It would be as though I was taking advantage ..."

She kissed him gently, sweetly, without passion. "Then I'll take advantage of you. Charles ... I'm going to call you that in private ... It took a little doing to make up my mind. Don't make me beg you."

He was stung to the quick. Oh lord ... I didn't realize ..." She kissed the confusion from him and a soft subtle movement made the blood pound furiously in his head.

She clasped her hands behind his head and leaned back from the waist up. "Do you know where my room is?"

"Er ... somewhere on the third floor, east wing, isn't it?"

"No, the other servants live there and there wasn't room for me. I'm at the very end of the west wing, third floor. All by myself ..." She released him and stepped back, her eyes reflective of a certain wistful longing, the need of affection and a desire for him that was measureless.

For the third time that day emotion quite overcame Charles Corbett Carraway, the Third, and through his dark, rather soulful eyes she became a servant transformed into a queen. So much she had done for his sore and lacerated spirit that this last capitulation of hers was more than his overloaded heart could stand and he fell forward to his knees and seized her about the legs, moving his face against the starched surface of her uniform.

"I'll never be able to tell you what you've done for me this night," he said with unconscious melodrama.

"I don't need telling," she said softly. She stroked his head with a gentle hand, then to his surprise she raised the hem of the uniform and lifted the most magnificent leg he had ever seen. Without thinking, he embraced it and kissed its satin surface. He could feel the rippling shudder that coursed through her and the marble surface of her skin became pebbly with chilling excitement.

"That," she said throatily, "was to make sure you'd come. What you did makes it certain that if you don't come to me, I'll come to you."

He stood up and a knot forced its way into his throat. "Edna ... please don't do this unless you want to."

She put her arms around him. "Can't you believe I want to? Can't you believe that I want to because I know you need me ... and I need you? Can't you believe that?"

He nodded, his throat too thick to answer. She released him. "In thirty minutes ..." And she was gone.

He sat in a richly upholstered chair and tried to focus his mind. He tried to find an answer for what had happened. Why had she acted as she had? A little clarity came to his mind. He needed someone like Edna sorely. She needed to be needed. With an insight that spoke of a kind of prescience she had sensed what she couldn't see. She had divined what she couldn't know. Hers was a wisdom born of the woman of acute sensitivity, perception, and a master of emotional mathematics. Freed of torment and remorse, Charles felt almost lightheaded with anticipation.

No personal moralist but full to the eyes with the more garish mores of the time, he had been successfully wrestled out of their grasp and was now free to partake and enjoy. He had paid the small voice of his conscience the demanded tribute and now it was silent. Again he felt a twinge of guilt. How easily she had routed his objections. What a peculiar position it was to be in, he, the male, protesting and she overcoming it rather easily. Ordinarily, it should be the other way around; however, had she not forced the issue she would still be the pleasant maid to whom he was accustomed like the drapes in the library. He recalled that he had never been a boudoir buccaneer, having been somewhat shy and retiring. There had been times, of course, but as in the case of Edna, it amounted to a situation whereby escape was difficult and on no account could his victory be laid to his own efforts. Deterred by disposition from becoming a love pirate, he had done a great deal of day dreaming wherein he became, in the dream, what he most definitely was not in life.

He was highly imaginative and if his own wife surpassed him in this department, it was because she took the initiative and his shyness persisting, he found himself outstripped at that one thing at which he should have excelled.

He took a leisurely, hot, tub bath and went to the little bar that housed a few bottles of liquor, usually used for an occasional nightcap. He took a stiff drink, then considered his not unattractive body in the mirror. His face was a good, rather square, one with several planes and sharp angles, on the strong side and given to immobility. This he knew to be a sham to cover up inner tensions, uncertainty and conflict.

He had succeeded as president of Carraway Chemicals but he was beginning to wonder if success was worth the pound of flesh it seemed bent on exacting as its price. His teeth were good and regular, and his hair once as black as a crow was beginning to silver richly at the temples.

Carraway Chemicals was largely the cause of the grey hair, he decided. The rest of his body, while still retaining the outlines that athletics had carved, was now padded and beginning to dimple in places. This irked him no end but he had resisted the usual executive sessions at a club with barbells, masseurs and the smooth assurances of some belly beater that he was never in better condition. He knew better.

CHAPTER TWO

On the broad verandah, Charles Corbett Carraway, the Third, roused himself from his reverie and started to get up and go to his room but his thoughts were too rosy. Edna, the fabulous Edna. He had been thinking of her and the occurrence last week. A sudden resolution came to him. He'd visit her again tonight, but first he'd tease himself further, thinking about the first night. Since that night he had thought of little else and these thoughts and the act had set the tiger free. This tiger was destined to spring out of concealment before long and Carraway Chemicals was in for a shock that would take some time to overcome.

Charles finished his narcissistic study and slipped on a robe, took it off. immediately and searched until he discovered one that he had never worn. It was of woolly white pile and it gave him the looks of being fifteen pounds heavier, broadened his shoulders and seemed to fit the occasion well. A ringing pang whipped through his stomach as he realized that now all that was to be done was to walk up one flight of steps, traverse the long west wing corridor, open the last door on the right and step into another world peopled by the unbelievable Edna.

He was sure that the room would have her own personality hanging from the drapes, from the flounces around her dressing table with her scrubbed, white soap cleanliness in the air, the pink and milk and gold wonder of her reflected in everything in the room. The bed would be big and soft and maybe show a slight depression where she had slept night after night. Her hair, once let down, would be shoulder length and maybe longer. It would billow about her shoulders and maybe down her back in dense, soft waves, like spun gold and softer than silk. He had already noticed that it was of fine caliber and heavy.

He tied the sash around his middle and stepped toward the door. It opened and Lavender stepped into the room. She had been to a dance ... with Dr. Floyd, no doubt, but now she was a wreck. That she had been in arid out of the evening dress was immediately apparent. Also apparent was the use to which she had put her lips. Lipstick was liberally smeared from cheeks to chin.

"Well ... if it isn't li'l Boy Blue ... Come blow your huck." She waved a languid hand before her face. "Par'n me," she said owlishly. "Blow your horn, blue boy ... Saaay are you blue? Y'look perfeckly virginal whi' ri' now." She stumbled and fell sprawling. "Dammit," she said irritably. "Look like y' could pig up y'r own li'l ever lovin' wife from off the floor." She sat up and crossed her legs.

"Where are your pants?" he asked, feeling amazingly cold and far away. He had asked the question out of surprise ... a matter he found considerably annoying. Why should he be surprised?

She looked at him blearily then down. She giggled. "Now where'n 'ell could they of gone d'ye suppose?"

"Maybe Floyd took them to his apartment and stuffed them."

She staggered to her feet and slid the dress over her head. After it came the half-slip. She wore no bra because nature had favored her with breasts that were as firm as cold butter. She was proud of the fact that she did not possess a bra. She sat on the bed and braced herself with both hands.

"Stuff my pants? They was stuffed all to hell'n gone when he got to 'em. Why'd he want to do that? He was after the stuffin' ... not the pants."

Charles felt the tug of nausea that rose in his throat but it disappeared. It was the last time he was to feel it.

"Gimme a dring," she ordered, looking sleepily at the small bar. Gimme a big dring and don't talk about Floyd. He's just like you. A good wringin' out and he caves in at the middle…" She giggled. Dammit, I want a man … a *real* man"

He poured her a drink that might have made a man pause but she poured it down and hiccoughed as the fumes came back. "Gimme a li'l water. Tryin' t' cut m' throat?"

He gave her the water. She started to drink it, dropped the glass, starting a little from the cold bite of the water as it deluged her middle.

"Col' …" she said dazedly. "Col' …" She fell backward on the bed, out for the night.

Charles tossed the spread negligently over her and walked out of the door He was still thinking about her when he stopped in front of Edna's door. Again trepidation and guilt knifed him through the middle and he leaned against the door facing for a moment to collect his courage … and the door opened in his face.

"I was coming," she said. "I saw her come in. I knew she was drunk, so I didn't think she'd give us any trouble."

He walked in and shook his head a little to clear the fumes of her presence from his head. She wore a housecoat of ankle length bronze slipper satin that zippered down the front. It might have been applied from the hips up with a paint gun, so urgently did it fit.

He put the bottle on her dressing table and said, "Edna, this must be right. Let's just let things take their appointed course, shall we?"

She nodded and came into his arms, heating him anew with the electric warmth of her body. No little heat was generated because of the knowledge that like him she wore nothing beneath the robe. She had bathed and as he had imagined her hair tumbled riotously to her shoulders in deep natural waves, silk soft and as bright as fine wires.

He kissed her and heard the trilling of a fundamental little song sound deep in her chest. He released her against his will, wishing to drag it out as long as he could … unconsciously afraid of this woman who was so much woman. He made them high-balls and they toasted each other with their eyes. Edna was not a drinker and soon she was flushed and her eyes sparkling with animation and something else that seemed like the pinpoint of flame announcing a slumbering volcano.

"I'm not good at female things," she said, her breasts heaving with ill-concealed emotion. "I mean maybe there is some way they have of being coy and mysterious and come-hitherish..." She looked up into his eyes and gripped him hard. "Charles, make me do what you want me to. I don't know much about things like this..." She bit her lip and her big blue eyes flooded with tears. "I'm doing it all wrong and I must sound like a fool but the truth is... Really, I never did before and now I'm fright-ened and unsure of myself."

"Do you want to call it off, Edna?" His voice had a sound that startled him. It was rich and assured. *She* was asking *him,* deferring to him, depending on his judgment, asking for his understanding. The change was first noticed in his voice. Conscious of the change now he felt like a giant, like a man of some savage tribe now accepted by his elders as one of them. He could carry a spear and dance around the fire to the drums... He stopped and led her to the couch that stood across the room.

"Shall we call it off?"

She sat down and leaned across him, pulling his head down to her lips. "No," she whispered as their lips came together and he knew she meant it.

When he could stand the racketing clamor set up by her lips he sat up and cradled her in his arms, looking at her as though expecting her to turn into something else... fearing that she might. Her body was restless now... abandoned was quiescence, abandoned was passivity. Charles thrilled to the core at the activ-ity. It was like a worm that did not know where to crawl, a mole that had lost its hole, active yet knowing and yet untutored, with none of Lavender's courtesan-seeking, with objectivity that left him following rather than leading.

"Charles…" the word was an entreaty to lead her further toward a goal with which she was not familiar… begging him for tutelage… offering her hand that he led her where she knew she should go but had never been.

With his left hand he caught the zipper and stripped it down, hissing a shrill tinny protest, then he leaned back and allowed that stunning witchery of her fabulous body to blast his senses and render him numb with delight. Still within the confines… within the boundaries of the robe she looked like a fabulous pink pearl offered by a mollusk that had opened its bivalves for the world to see what nature had wrought. With an animal sound he caught her and lifted her from her shell… It trailed and caught on her feet, slipping lubricously from her back-thrown arms… then falling from her feet to the floor, leaving her in the flesh, vibrant, somewhat frightened, tense with wanting and waiting… all of her all of his… waiting for him to take the fruit of her offering, yet not able to help… or maybe unwilling for fear of performing some wrongful or clumsy act.

Her breath came rapidly as he stood up, as the robe finally gave up. She was light as a feather to him and yet he knew she wasn't Gently he stood her on her feet and his mouth delved deeply again. Acquiescence was gone and in its place came a blind seeking and her hands beneath his robe roved like mice lost in the dark… and it came open and the primordial heat that was a fever in her reached him and returned to the giant his power.

She was a fragrant incensory, emanating that most priceless of all perfumes, a woman clean and vibrant with woman's most exalted emotion, wanting her choice of man with the all-giving desire that is immeasurable, unbelievable.

Her hair spread out on the white pillow and though there were things she did not know there were others which were her birthright as a woman… then a kind of frenzied panic came on and sent a convulsion through her. Her hands seized his face, close above hers, and her breath rasped out rapidly and forcefully.

"Charles…please be gentle with me." A look of fearful despair clouded her eyes. "Oh, Charles. please make me what you want…but be gentle with me." A frown furrowed her forehead and her body tensed electrically…her breathing stopped for one agonizing second, then the frown gradually erased itself, her face smoothed out its taut lines and a trembling smile touched her lips and a throaty little growl came from the depths of her chest.

"Ahh-h-h-h-h-h…*Charles.*"

Charles Corbett Carraway, the Third, had no friends of the sort that men get drunk with, share their dirty little secrets, discuss a common enemy or have bouts of weeping affection while in their cups. In fact, Charles was awash with emotions and impulses that had been trodden and contained for so long that the breaking point was near. His physician, a kindly man, whose knowledge of medicine was merely a tool with which to manipulate his knowledge of humanity, had tried to get him to unload some of the debris that clogged his soul. Charles had had a sudden desire to tell all but before he could get started the old inhibitions returned and he shrank from baring his inner self. Physicians, being for the greater part, men, failed where Edna Ivorsen had succeeded, having only herself as apparatus. It was more than enough. Charles, while under her stupefying charm, had watched a film strip of his life and how frustrating it was.

Charles, feeling better, got up from the porch chair and walked down the steps, down the driveway until he came to the ragged gash in the shrubbery that marked the passage of the Thunderbird. He got in the car, started it and backed it out of the green tangle and drove it into the garage. In the light reflected back from the white interior and except for a few spots of sap, the car had taken no damage. Charles got out and closed the door, feeling somewhat virtuous that his silly impulse had not caused any damage.

He stopped and closed his hands tightly. What if he had caused damage? The car was his, the house was his, the shrubbery was his ... It was about time he started thinking of himself in the present, singular. On an impulse he looked up and saw a light in an upper story window. A feeling of warm well being swept over him and he entered the house from the back. Lavender, of course, was out and that suited him fine.

Edna was in bed reading. She wore a shorty nightgown that was so thin as to be practically non-exist-ant, and when he opened the door she gasped and rolled over protectively. She saw it was him, relaxed and smiled her slow, cat-like smile.

"Hello," she said huskily. She stretched like a tigress and seemed to virtually crawl out of the thin garment from all angles and ends. He came and sat on the side of the bed, and let his hand slide gently over a round shoulder. She shuddered and leaned against him. Her soft mouth playing with the skin of his neck. She raised her face and brought her lips to his, shattering him with the old voltage that he had now come to expect, but she sensed something different.

"You're thinking," she said, leaning against him the twin bulges of her breasts resting warmly against his chest.

"I guess I am. Edna, what does a man do who has come to the end of a rope?"

She shrugged. "You're being vague but ... Well, maybe I do know what you're talking about. Last week you had come to the end of another rope." She caressed his face and kissed him with gentle pressure. "I helped then, didn't I?"

"You saved my reason," he said, his voice thick with feeling. "What would I have done without you?"

"Let's don't think about that. There was me and if you think I didn't need you, too, you're mistaken."

"Why?"

She kissed him again and smiled in the midst of it, giving him a novel sensation. She rubbed her nose against his and withdrew a little.

"Haven't you ever wanted to be supremely important ... not to business or anything ... just to a woman? A woman, not necessarily that you love, because I don't think you love me. Just to a woman to whom you feel close, with whom you feel free ... a person it was good to be around, comfortable and no strain. Haven't you ever wanted that?"

"I've wanted that. Last week and three times since I've had it. Unless you stop me, I'll have it again tonight."

She nodded and gently stripped the robe from his shoulders, caressing the good smooth skin with delicate fingers.

"Then maybe you've answered your own question. Don't you think in my own way I've felt everything you have ... maybe more? It's more important to a woman to feel wanted ... necessary. Think how I felt the next morning lying here in bed with you, watching you breathe and sleep so softly, so relaxed like a baby ... no tensions, no bitter memories and more important, no remorse."

"Did you feel any?"

"I suppose a virgin always does the first time ... for a while, but if she makes it all right in her own mind, she gets over it. You see, I was never beaten over the head with moral whips. I knew too much about life and nature to ever become ridden downhill by morals. I think my father had about the soundest moral outlook I ever saw and I think mother reflected it. Bodies around our house were never dirty unless at the end of a hard and sweaty day and that was taken care of in the bathroom. I can remember what my father looked like ... in fact, I can't remember not knowing. And my two brothers ... we always went around the house in all stages of dress and undress and no one ever seemed to think it was wrong. In fact, no one ever seemed to think anything whatever about it. We all sort of drifted gradually into some vague sense of mature privacy and the boys or my father never smoked their pipes in the living room in the nude."

She giggled and continued: "I'm afraid I was the worst about that. I remember one of the *brethren* came in one afternoon unannounced and caught me stretched on the couch reading a book. It had been hot and I had taken a cold bath and stretched out without thinking about anything but comfort. Well, this vise-jawed old man came in ... he was a sort of unofficial general hell-firer for the community and probably the nastiest-minded old blue nose that ever walked. We're a good, solid, home-loving, good eating, hard drinking, Swedish-Norwegian-Danish-German community, at home. Mostly Lutheran or Calvinist ... generally pretty tolerant and let-live people who had a good understanding of life and nature and how it behaves. The youngsters misbehave about like everywhere else when they think they can get away with it and the parents smile up their sleeve, look the other way and feel that most of the time things will come out all right as, of course, they do. Well, the old boy got his eyeful that afternoon. I can see him now swelling up like a poisoned pup and glaring at me. I sat up, shocked, I can tell you, because our freedom was a family thing, not for outsiders, but I had to either run or look like a fool ..."

"Oh," said Charles laughing, "sit there and look like no angel his narrow old mind could have ever conceived."

She nodded. "So I told him that mother and father were in the kitchen ... and I sat there and looked back at him just as bold as all get out and he finally wilted and sneaked out to the kitchen. I got up, went to my room and dressed. Then I sneaked back and listened to hell break loose in the kitchen. He was giving father and mother down the country for allowing their daughter to loll around in the house, an open invitation to rape. Then my father, who's a pretty easy-going, tolerant sort, stood up and just about blasted him out of the kitchen. He told him that people didn't ordinarily go around entering other people's houses without knocking and if he did and got an eyeful he should be thankful that he got to see something like me once before he died and that if he heard any more about it or if it got talked around the country, he'd personally beat seventeen kinds of awful things, including fertilizer, out of him."

Charles laughed freely and leaned back against a pillow and the headboard of the bed.

"So ended the only attempt to make a blushing maiden out of you."

"So it ended. Father did mildly suggest that in the future I'd better watch how I displayed myself because as he put it I was becoming about as fetchin' a heifer as had ever run the Ivorsen range and he didn't want me enticing maverick bulls around the place." She sat straight, her high proud breasts punching twin tents in the thin cloth of her gown. "So you see, I might have had some little twinges because it was the first time, but they were all gone when I saw what I had been able to do for you."

"And what did I do for you?"

She spanked his cheek smartly. "Oh … you men. Don't you know *anything*? Don't you know what those nights have meant to me and don't you know what a careless, uncaring, clumsy, rough-house man can do to a woman … especially that first time?" She lunged forward and crushed him back against the headboard. "Charles …" her eyes filled with tears. "Can't you see how wonderful you were for me?"

He took her face in his hands and looked at her carefully. "No, I can only see what you were for *me*."

A sob caught in her throat and she seemed to envelop him with soft-strong arms, presenting him a palpitant breast like a votive offering to a deity. Her hair came down over his face smothering him in its silken wonder, perfumed with the essence of clean woman untouched by artifice or commercial fragrance.

He took a deep breath, then gasped in shocked wonder. She raised her face, looked at him with staring eyes, more shocked than his own, her body taut with achievement, the ease and suddenness of which had surprised them.

As he had seen before, the tenseness abated gradually and the smile came to her face, a smile of delirious victorious joy and he relaxed, giving himself over to her strength, her suppleness, and the orgiastic eagerness of her love.

CHAPTER THREE

Dawn found them still entangled just where nature had dropped them through the veil of sleep. Her face was close to his and her breath was sweet on his cheek. Simultaneously their eyes opened and simultaneously they smiled. He kissed her fleetingly and sat up. He looked down at her, twisted now in a stretch like a well-rested cat, graceful ... even more so in contortion, so heartbreakingly lovely that his eyes stung and his breast grew tight. A sudden resolution reached him. He got up and put on his robe. "Come here, I have an announcement to make."

She sat up. "Do I have to dress?"

"No. I did so out of habit. Stand up."

He took her into his arms and holding her close said, "Edna, will you marry me as soon as I'm free?"

Her mouth drew down at the corners and her eyes were deeply serious. "No, Charles," she said in a voice that was mother soft. "I won't marry you."

He was thunderstruck for a moment. "But why, Edna? You must feel something for me ..."

"Of course, I do. In fact, I love you."

"Then ..."

"Sit down, Charles, and let me talk to you."

He sat down feeling a crushing poisonous disappointment that hurt physically.

She took his hands and folding them, placed them between her breasts. The gesture heightened the terrible ache and he felt his eyes growing damp.

"I've meant a great deal to you lately. Because I'm like I am and because no man was ever more in need of what I could provide. Affection…yes, love after a fashion. In your need it has mounted in importance. Love shouldn't be conceived in a case of such need. Too many woman could have done the same thing that I did. Maybe they wouldn't have been as vocal as I because I'm fairly well educated and I've done mountains of reading. I think I have a sense of the dramatic and a little knowledge of a certain particular brand of good taste. I was, in a sense, a full Christmas tree with all the trimmings when you'd have been satisfied with a stocking hung by the chimney. Now it has gotten the best of you. Although I can understand you, feel a great affection for you, give whatever you desire of me and of my body…and although my heart tells me that this is love, I know my heart is echoing something that you started that first night. I'm afraid I'm a little like girls in the old country. Love is something that might or might not accompany a marriage. That sort of idea makes Americans uneasy and resentful. It's against all their storybook ideas, against what they're fed on the radio and TV. It's something that shouldn't be and it offends them." She dropped his hands and let them slide down her flanks to rest on the marble smooth crests of her thighs.

"When I've had enough of this…" She spread her hands and looked around the room. "I'll go back to Nebraska and marry some nice, solid farmer with land and maybe some money and we'll rear a fine family of well-fed, uninhibited children who'll run naked around the house until someday they'll realize they're grown and people just don't do that."

Charles tore the stricture from his throat. "And you won't love this man?"

"I very likely will. I intend to go to college a couple of years because one finds a better type of man there. I wanted to see the rich thickly settled, East Coast. That's why I'm here. I want to see Midwestern college life. That's why I'm going." She leaned forward. "Charles, can you understand a farm girl wanting to do all these things?"

He nodded. "Yes, I can. What I wonder is what started this idea in your head."

"My mother...she was a college graduate. A school teacher when Father married her. She told me of all the wonderful things to see. The big houses, people with money..."

"She didn't think anything would happen to you?"

"She *knew* something would happen to me." She leaned forward and gave him a close-up of her lovely face. "Something has, Charles. Something so wonderful that no matter what happens to me in the future, I'll always remember you with all the love I feel now." A faraway look came into her eyes as she looked unseeingly out of the window. "Now, I think I'll go home. I've had my experience, I've seen how this side lives."

"You won't stay and marry me?"

"No, Charles. I could come up to your standard of living but you couldn't come down to mine. I like mine and the only thing I like about yours is you." She caught his hands and stroked her thighs with them. "I wonder if you know how many passes I've ducked since I've been here?"

"No."

"Dozens. Hardly a day without anywhere from one to several. I also know Miss Lavender told Dr. Carmicheal to trip me in the shrubbery and stop eating me with his eyes. She offered to get me drunk if she could, so I'd be easy."

"Oh, my God," he burst out disgustedly. "Carmicheal is fifty years old."

She smiled. "And a very nice old gentleman. In fact, it was he who told me."

"*No.*"

"Yes. It was late one night and Miss Lavender had kept me up to serve the stragglers. He came back into the kitchen. He was a little drunk. He paid me extravagant compliments, said I was the most beautiful woman he had ever seen and how did I manage to work for the most unregenerate bitch ever whelped and a lot more. He told me that I made his heart beat dangerously fast...for his age, that he wanted me like no one he'd ever seen but that he'd not touch a woman young enough to be his grand-daughter. He said he admired me and that if I ever needed anything for any purpose whatever I was to consider it ready and waiting."

Charles laughed with relief. "I always had a lot of affection for the old goat. That's just about what I'd expect from him."

He stood up. "Well, before we set tongues to wagging, I'd better go. I'll go on hoping, though...and I understand, Edna...I want you to know that."

"Thanks," she said throatily, and got to her feet. She opened his robe, stepped into the breach and closed it about her. She lifted her face to an inch of his lips and her body made her words unnecessary. "Don't go yet."

"Hell," he said with a laugh that was crazy. "I don't know if I'll go at all."

It was a long time before he left and when he got to his own room Lavender was sitting up in bed having coffee.

"Where in the hell have you been all night and why didn't Edna bring my coffee? Julius had to bring it and he spilled half the pot on the way."

He looked at her coolly and took a chair by the little bedside table, poured himself a cup of coffee. He sipped the scalding brew appreciatively.

"Am I supposed to know where Edna is?"

She waved a languid hand. "I was just making talk..." She started and looked at him. "Come to think of it maybe you do know where she is...It's a thought, although I can bet she was disappointed."

"You offered to set her up for Carmicheal. What's wrong with me taking a shot at it? You've lost interest in my abilities as a Romeo."

"You never had any abilities as a Romeo," she told him coldly, "but I won't have anything like that in my house ... right under my nose. Did you or didn't you spend the night with Edna?"

"He did," said Edna, calmly, as she wheeled the coffee wagon in. "I'm sorry I was late but that might happen anytime like it did this morning. I thought you might like some fresh coffee."

Lavender was so outraged that she spilled coffee on a hundred dollar negligee ... one of her cheaper ones.

"Well, that is about as brazen as you can get," she shrilled. "You're fired as of this minute. Tell Carrick to write you a check."

"Oh, no." Charles took a sip of coffee and lit a cigarette.

"What do you mean, 'Oh, no'," snapped Lavender. "I said she's fired and she's fired."

"Oh, no," he said, calmly, repetitious.

"What the devil are you maundering about?"

"Just what I said. You said she's fired, I say she isn't."

Lavender became calm. "You sleep with my maid and brazenly tell me about it. She, with more brass than a saloon cuspidor confirms it and you say 'Oh, no'. Get wise, sonny. Either she goes or word'll get around."

Charles chuckled and poured more coffee with a steady hand. "You're really amusing, Lavender," he said quietly. "Tell you what. I'll agree to a bargain. You fire all those women I've been sleeping with and I'll fire ..." His eyes grew hard. "Those like Dr. Floyd that you've been rolling around with."

Lavender almost fainted and Edna, forgetting for a moment that she was a lady's maid let go with a bray of cornfed laughter that was straight from the plains of Nebraska.

Charles sipped coffee and took a drag from his cigarette. "Is it a bargain?"

Lavender, who had conceived an early contempt for the mild mannered puppy she married because of his money and other less important matters, was stunned. That anything she had done had been noticed by her husband did not fit into the picture she had held of him for a long time. He was a fool, a goop who went around only partly conscious except at board meetings and at his office. She had pulled the yam over his eyes, but good, and now to suddenly be faced with the fact that he wasn't such a goop after all was a shock that came at a bad time. She was still shaky from her night's bout with bed and bottle, and her thoughts were hard to order.

Charles got up and escorted Edna to the door. "Forget it," he said gently. "When you get ready to go, let me know. In the meantime try to change your mind in my favor ... please."

Her eyes were melting and she squeezed his hand. "No, Charles. Don't expect it. I'll let you know ... and ..." The pleading in her eyes was unmistakable.

He nodded. "Every possible chance ... every possible one."

She squeezed his hand again and disappeared down the hallway.

The break ... It had come and Charles couldn't remember when he had felt so lighthearted and exultant. He walked over to a desk and took out a sheaf of eight by ten prints and flung them to his wife as she sat stricken on the bed, a dark spot plastered to her stomach where the coffee had soaked her gown and negligee.

"Take a look at those, my dear, and tell me whether we shall have a quiet, 'incompatible' type of divorce or one of those woolly whistlers that make a sordid laundromat out of some local courtroom to the intense glee of the various press organizations."

They had scattered rather well and Lavender, unable to sort them out, got quite a nice eyeful of herself in some garishly revealing situations. Whoever the infra-red photographer had been, he knew what he was about and had done his job to a high degree of proficiency ... and all in a week. Charles looked at her white, stricken face and wondered what sort of collection he might have had if he'd started sooner. He had saved one and when he thought the moment ripe, he tossed the final bombshell in her lap. Dr. Floyd was her partner this time and she had

29

evidently convinced him that he was a hopeless blunderer, a man of no imagination and little talent because he was displaying in this picture a versatility and variety consciousness that was something to see. Lavender, herself, not to be caught wanting, was performing in a manner that left no doubt as to the extent of her own inventiveness. She took one look and keeled over sideways in the bed.

He looked at her drawn white face passionlessly, picked up his prints and locked them in the desk.

Dr. Carmicheal was a man of many minds and talents. He had been a chemist, a clergyman, a deck hand, a soldier, a rider of the stock market, and finally after adventure had palled somewhat, he settled into respectability and became a business man. His qualities of leadership and his knowledge of the market were such that he had achieved the presidency of Carraway Chemicals when. Charles Corbett Carraway, the Second, had died and held it until Charles Corbett, the Third, returned from the battlefields of the far east. Then Carmicheal relinquished the reins to the Crown Prince and went upstairs as chairman of the board where he managed to annoy a great many people and had a fine time for himself.

He had never quite understood the younger Carraway but having understood the elder two a little too well, he made the necessary calculation and hit the nail squarely the first blow. The other two had been fine business men with a certain hardheaded piratical streak in them at a time when such piracy was the thing in industrial circles, softened when times changed and flourished.

Charles Corbett, the Third, had been reared without the slightest regard for his own opinions or impulses. It was written that he'd one day succeed to the presidency of Carraway Chemicals and to question it would have been the most callous heresy. No one had, least of all Charles Corbett, the Third. Now Charles Corbett was president and not overly happy about it.

Carmicheal made further calculations, listened, got drunk at the president's house, listened to and watched the president's wife and came to other fairly accurate conclusions.

Miss Agatha Mimms, Dr. Carmicheal's confidential secretary, could and had stood most things that any confidential secretary has to stand. She took them like spring steel and bounded back for more. She was spare, unlovely, ascetic and carping. Dr. Carmicheal enjoyed her because he could always be sure of an argument.

"The boy ain't happy," he said one day half an hour before a board meeting.

"Why ain't he?" she mimicked with a frown.

"Hell, how do I know except he wasn't ever cut out to be a president ... does a fair job, of course, with me to advise him.."

Miss Mimms laughed sarcastically and snapped her thin lips shut tightly.

"Er ..." He looked at her over his glasses, his craggy over-nosed face harshed. "None of your lip, Aggie. I could fire you, you know."

"Sure, and you'd have me back in ten minutes to find your glasses."

"Ummm ... well ... By the way, where are they?"

"On that breathing appendage you have which under less stimulated circumstances might be called a nose."

"Oh ... Yes, so they are ... and let my nose alone. Well, like I say, he ain't happy."

"I heard you the first time. What's eatin' you?"

Dr. Carmicheal twisted his six foot plus frame of slim but still erect bones about in his chair.

"Don't know exactly. But I'm afraid the boy'll get all fouled up one of these days ... By gosh, if I'd had his money at his age you'd never've got me tied to a swivel chair and a pack of fool directors and ..."

"You're one of 'em."

"So I am. The biggest fool of the lot likely." He sighed. "Never did go back to Rapa Iti that time ... By gosh, she was tall and slim as a switch, milky brown and with a butt like a hundred dollar cow. Chested up like the cliffs of Dover and twitch to her middle that ..."

"Dr. ... *Carmicheal* ..."

"Oh ... er, pardon me, Aggie. Just sort of mulling over unfinished business. Now I'm fifty, she's fifty with a stern as broad as a bale of cotton and nineteen grandchildren. She'll weigh close to three hundred pounds."

"Spare me your bawdy reminiscences," she snapped sharply.

"Oh, come now. You should have lived some adventure. Might threaten you with a red blood corpuscle or something."

Miss Mimms lifted her nose. "Oh, I know you think I'm nothing but a dried up old maid with nothing but a couple of sachet bundles for my memories but I'll tell you something, in my youth I was a *thing*. I could curl your hair, you tottering neat septuagenarian."

"Now, now. I meant no offense and I'll bet in your time you were a wiggle-middle of no mean ... er wiggle."

Miss Mimms' eyes misted over. "Oh, shut up. I could still pull your plug, Buster, if I was half a mind."

"Now, Aggie, I've apologized. Don't make me take you up on that."

She let loose a single derisive, *"Hah,"* and turned back to her typewriter.

Dr. Carmicheal answered the knock on the door. "Come in." It was Charles and the look on his face was strangely comforting to the old man. Something was about to happen. He could think of any number of things that needed happening but whatever it was, if it was sufficiently annoying to the greatest possible number of people, then Dr. Carmicheal was for it. To him people who could be annoyed were fair game. It was applause from mediocre minds.

"Don't look so serious," said Dr. Carmicheal in opposition to the way he felt. "Have a seat."

"No, thank you," said Charles tightly. "Will you attend the board meeting this morning?"

"Don't I generally ... me being chairman and all that?"

"Yes, of course, but this morning I particularly want you there. Better borrow a few bottles of smelling salts, too, and fetch them along."

"Why, somebody gonna faint?"

"Most likely. See you in a few minutes."

Dr. Carmicheal watched him stalk through the door and wriggled his prominent nose. "Now that's the first time I ever saw that lad walk like he was going somewhere. Did you notice his voice, Aggie?"

"Yes. Sounded like a man talking, not that apologetic mutter he usually uses."

"You're unusually perceptive this morning. My compliments."

She made a face at him and went back to her work.

"I think he spoke plainly enough," said Dr. Carmicheal in answer to the stuttered, amazed questions that followed the silence that followed Charles Corbett Carraway's announcement that effective today he was no longer a member of the organization.

"Very plain. He's quittin'. It's that simple."

One man, whose amazement had not dimmed his business sense, wanted to know, "But what about the stock ... your stock. Are you just going to sit on it ... and who'll get the proxy?"

Charles knew that was what was worrying him. "I'm sitting on it. I'll give the proxy to Dr. Carmicheal and if you're smart you'll put him back in my chair."

Dr. Carmicheal refrained from laughter with difficulty. This was the most enjoyable meeting he'd attended in a long time. Everyone was annoyed and not a few of the more conservative element were downright dismayed. Charles, having dropped his bombshell, turned and walked from the room ... again as though he had somewhere to go. In this particular instance he did. Edna was waiting.

Dr. Carmicheal stood up. "Well, we'd just as well shelve current business until we elect someone to fill that chair."

"That's right," said the first vice-president who had an eye on the chair and of all the rest he had recovered from his astonishment quickest. "Whom shall it be?"

"I have a suggestion," said Dr. Carmicheal. "I have no intention of beating my brains out in the position but for this once I'll sit in and we can dispose of the business at hand and then turn to the matter of the presidency. Just don't consider me at all.

"What's the matter, J. J.," asked the second vice-president, "you getting old?"

"No," said Carmicheal blandly, "but I don't intend to let the chair make me old. In fact, the boy has given me an idea."

CHAPTER FOUR

Shayne Bennett was not, as her name suggested, a boy. Maybe she should have been but nature conspired against her and gave her a body that would not have suited a boy. Shayne was a rebel and lived during a time when rebels were allowed to rebel with more grace and less interference than her mother who was also a rebel and took it out on various members of her family and the public in general. She was accounted a little nuts and certainly someone to stay clear of. She, like Shayne, was clean cut and long of limb, athletic but also feminine to no small degree.

She had buried one husband who had found it hard to keep up with her, who never understood what went on behind his wife's high, intelligent forehead. He accepted the high voltage living that she forced upon him and floundered, as it were, in her wake much like a small boat towed at high speed behind a lean and daring cruiser. He learned not to struggle against the inevitable and at the age of forty died of a heart ailment which people said had been aggravated, if not wholly caused, by his wife's speed of living.

She married again, a Mr. Archibald Denny, a dour man of violent religious convictions, jaundiced outlook, and a completely distorted opinion of the worth of his own son by another wife. Why a lover of life, an intellectual and a woman who lived at a torrid pace ever married Archibald Denny no one ever quite understood. Public understanding is often lacking in such ill-suited marriages. It soon became apparent that Mr. Denny would not survive many years of life with Marian because she simply sucked him along in her wake just as she had her first husband, but where Frank Bennett bowed to the inevitable and went along for the ride, Archibald Denny went but he went protesting bitterly every step of the way. It made him lose weight and develop an ulcer. It made his entrails curdle when his good money went to buy such examples of the demon rum as was fancied by Marian and her social set.

Shayne had too much of Marian in her, in fact more than the mother could cope with and she gave up early. This compromise enabled her and her daughter to establish a deep affectionate understanding that was based on nothing but mutual respect and the usual parent-child relationship had to take a back seat. Archibald's adopted son Marvin, a lad Shayne's age, managed to stay somewhat in the background, enjoyed his father's discomfiture just as he enjoyed anyone's discomfiture. Marvin had been taught early that he was a very special person. Marvin also had just the temperament to begin at that particular landing and work up. He was callous, sadistic, and utterly uncaring for a living person other than himself. Archibald was not particularly intelligent and Marvin could and did deceive his father so completely that it was no longer a challenge to his cleverness.

Archibald, had he been fairly smart, might have seen what he was getting into when he married Marian. He might even have had an inkling of why he married her. The fact that he was flattened by physical attraction one night when he saw her emerge from a midway side show and get her skirt blown over her head was never allowed to creep into his consciousness because such things were beneath his moral standards.

The reasons he admitted to were that she was a child of God, fast, drifting toward the dungeons of the devil. If it was necessary to marry her to save her, he was willing to be the martyr. That a sweet, suffocating pain had attacked him just beneath the breast bone when he saw the exorbitant length of her delightfully tanned legs all the way to the splash of silk that did little to obscure the rich expanse of her middle, was a matter that never reached him.

Not even on the day of the wedding when he was called upon to exert every milligram of will he possessed to keep from going into a nervous convulsion because the wedding party dragged interminably and he was anxious ... in fact, he was virtually slavering at the mouth to get about the business of saving her immortal soul. So eager and hungry was he that he was in agony to begin the saving process and became somewhat cross when, in the privacy of the hotel room, she insisted on a great many things not directly related to soul saving, the Denny way.

When at long last body and spirit were served, Archibald, like many of his mental ilk, simply wallowed in a slough of remorse, remembering in much too clear detail that he had performed abominably ... he had lost his head completely ... he had kissed her in unlikely places and had become a dog ... an animal ... any sort of animal in whom the mating urge is all powerful.

Marian had watched him from her place on the bed, nude, sated, surprised to some degree that he had turned out to be something she had not even suspected. She watched him on his knees, his head bowed while he wrestled with his soul and poured out agonizing supplication. She was grateful that his outpouring was not vocal. That she could not have stood. It was enough that she had to watch a man begging forgiveness for being a man. It was then that she began to wonder if she had done the right thing when she married him.

He got up, cleansed somewhat, and ordered her to put on her nightgown and henceforward it would be a decent garment of heavy muslin and not the thing she had worn briefly to bed. She looked at him in amazement for a moment, then uttered an unladylike word. She got up and walked over to him, her body undulating like a courtesan. She snatched open his virtuously tied robe and immersed him in the wonder of her body. As before, he fell before the assault and she was pardonably annoyed when he went through the same routine, punctuating his prayer this time with heavy, masculine sobs.

'Let me ask you one thing," she said after he had crawled weakly into bed, hugging the far edge as closely as possible. "Isn't this night's performance no more or less than par for the marital course?"

"It is for procreation alone," he said primly. "I lost my head. I acted abominably. I allowed passion to get the better of me. It was a Hell dance in this room with the devil calling the turns. Sex is a spiritual thing that is beautiful in the eyes of the Lord. Ours was not that. It was a sensuous orgy and it will have to stop."

"I'm sure it will," she said sarcastically. "I've just had a good example of how spiritual it is to you." Out of sheer perverseness she rolled over to him. She felt the leap of his muscles and the shudder that followed some shameless exploration on her part. He rolled over and grabbed her like a drowning man. She put a cool hand over his avid mouth.

"Now let's see how spiritual you can keep it."

He was a crushed man but there would be many more times like this and none but what held some new and more torturing elements.

Once when he thought he was drinking nothing any more alcoholic than a lemonade and discovered after it was too late that it had been rather liberally adulterated with gin, he quite outdid himself after company had gone home. So appallingly animal did he become that he spent days in spiritual anguish which she did little to assuage. One of her pet digs was to compliment him on his nocturnal activities and the amazing versatility which he could display at times.

However, it was Marian who went first to the grave ... in a messy car accident and left Shayne to Archibald's tender care. Immediately he set out to change her life and just as quickly did she let him know in terms that even he could understand, that her life, to whatever extent she could manage, was her own.

That Marvin also did about as he pleased did not reach through the fog of paternal devotion which the father lavished upon the adopted son. Archibald was not aware of it but the daughter was even more upsetting to his senses than had been the mother...a matter for which he had not been charitable enough to forgive even beyond the grave. It was just another weakness which Archibald adjusted to suit the demands of his psyche.

Things grew worse and on one occasion Archibald had the police in on the matter which shocked Shayne into just what she had to deal with. In a private session with juvenile Judge Cross, Shayne loosed a barrage of logic which left that amiable jurist reeling in his chair.

"Let's look at the thing this way," she had said. "I'm seventeen years old. I'd be out of high school but I broke three ribs one summer, high diving, and I lost a year because of some complications. I've never given the police any trouble. I've never been in any trouble. Yet three months after my mother dies this...jerk calls the police in. Where did they find me?"

Judge Cross harrumphed gently and looked at the steeple he had built of his fingers and wondered if the gesture was judicial enough. "Er...umm. I believe at the skating rink."

"Correct. I was not missing. I was not even skating with a boy." She tapped the paper before them. "I think he suggested to the officer in charge of the search that I might be found out with a man, doing much more than even skating on thin ice."

"Er...yes." The cold approach was getting on Judge Cross' nerves. No teen-ager should be this assured, this vocal. "Your father made some such suggestion."

"That's just like him. Do you know what he did when he took the wedding roll with my mother?"

The judge winced, then blushed. "Umm...no. What?"

"Got up and prayed. Said he'd been guilty of base passions or some such guff."

Oddly, Judge Cross wanted to laugh. He had had an interview with Archibald Denny and emerged from it a victim of a considerable mass of warring reactions. Denny had not been very impressive, his accusations the rankest nonsense and his intentions rather obscure. Obviously, he wanted the girl punished and had even mentioned the detention home. After discreet inquiries, Judge Cross realized that he had quite a problem on his hands, not the least of which was one Archibald Denny.

Still he was in a poor position to ignore a mature man who by some was accounted a pillar of the community, if by others a fool. He had had to throttle an impulse to agree with the latter group. He couldn't afford to take sides in a matter like this, no matter how strong his impulses. Judge Cross demolished his digital steeple and felt a vague sense of accomplishment. He leaned forward and loosed his personality.

"Tell me something about the boy... your stepbrother by adoption."

"Marvin ...? Oh, he's a whreep."

"Are ... er, your relations pleasant?"

"He goes his way and I go mine."

"No clashes?"

"Once I had to slap the ..." She stopped and allowed a slight smile to turn up the corner of her generous mobile mouth ... Whey out of him. Came in the bathroom and put his hands on me. That I don't allow. I didn't have much of anything on."

The judge cleared his throat and looked at his watch. Time was running out but he intended to get a full knowledge of what this household was like.

"Just what *did* you have on?"

"Well ... to be truthful, nothing."

"And the bathroom door was open?"

"Yes."

"Then might I suggest that it wasn't such a good idea?"

Shayne turned loose a smile that shook the judge severely and made his heart thump.

"I guess it wasn't but what the hell? Mamma and I used to parade all over the house in our nothings. We were never ashamed of our bodies. I never thought of Marvin as a man. To me, he's just a part of the furniture."

"Marvin's maturing," he suggested tentatively. "So, may I add, are you."

"Yes, I guess so. Mamma said one of these days I was going to have a rape shape."

The judge who had been secretly toying with a similar conclusion found to his intense irritation that he was blushing again. "Miss Bennett..." He stopped. He didn't know how to go on because he was about to exceed judicial license. He sat back and looked at her for a moment. She looked back with her enormous oblique green eyes. Her hair was parted in the middle and rubber banded into two luxuriant ponytails. It was brown...a tawny, golden brown with copper lights. It was so fine that he knew she had trouble with it. Possibly the reason for the simple coiffure. The eyes looked back, without guile, without coquettishness, without challenge. If this girl was a delinquent, then he'd never seen one. Of course she was bold...rather free in her reactions. She was modern and had been reared by a modem mother. Judge Cross knew more than a little about Marian Bennett and in this knowledge was a much greater understanding of the girl.

"Miss Bennett, will you walk to the door, then back here to your chair?"

She stood with a peculiarly fluid grace, whipped about and strode purposefully to the door, turned and walked back. Judge Cross blinked and held his face carefully wooden. Never in all his long years had he seen such a body. If it had a flaw it was the muscularity which was as fine and strong as a trained athlete's. If such could be called a flaw, her waist was maybe a shade too slim which accentuated the nubile swell of her hips. If it could be called a flaw, her breasts lunged too valorously against whatever she wore by way of restraint. They might be too high, too sharp, too assertive. Her legs, the way they moved beneath the material of her skirt … too smooth, too suggestive that even though they were covered they were nude. Her calves were too smooth, too finely done and her ankles too small.

Judge Cross suddenly grew angry with himself. What he had been doing was ticking off the girl's points of excellence and criticizing them. What if they were, too … everything. Wasn't the world built on exaggeration? If she were a little exaggerated, wasn't also Feary's world famous paintings of nudes exaggerated? Was it not a scheme of nature to inflate to the maximum in order to attract? Wasn't every woman three months' pregnant at the most beautiful time of her life?

Judge Cross mentally placed himself in the cubicle he reserved for fools. It was, he told himself, impossible to be objectively judicial with this girl. He shook invisible hands with himself. Was it not a part of justice to leave no stone unturned in the search for facts? Was he confusing justice with the law? In court one was given no alternative. A higher court would not look at justice but how the law had been administered. This was not district court. His place was to advise, to prevent, to make sure that tender girls and boys were not treated as criminals. He sentenced youths to the school of correction with the greatest reluctance, knowing that what began as a prank might, under the tutelage of habitual criminals, turn into something much worse. He realized that the state schools for delinquents were often colleges for crime.

Judge Cross came out of his reverie with a snap. She was still standing there looking at him, her inscrutable amber-green eyes still cool, calm and frank.

"You know, sometimes I think I can read minds," she said as she saw that he was with her again. Judge Cross then performed the climax of all his afternoon of blushes and silently cursed as he felt it mount to his face. For some reason he, too, felt that she could read minds but he must know.

"Really?" It was a hollow, unconvincing sound. He repeated it and felt better.

"Yes. I think basically you're a good man. You are in a sort of spot here and you don't like it. You made me walk to the door so you could see ... as well as you could, just what sort of temptation Marvin had."

Cross wished he was somewhere else. Nothing in this interview had gone right. He knew that at the end of it he would very likely do something foolish. He was not a man given to foolishness. There was no place for it on the bench. Yet, he was mortally certain that if some grave injustice was not meted out to this beautiful child, he would be found doing legal handsprings and the prospect offended his orderly mind.

"Yes, my dear, I think you read the old man's mind pretty well. I must admit that I was curious on my own account when I asked you to walk to the door. I might have told myself that I was being thorough or something ..." He laughed uncertainly. "I was not disappointed, no matter my reasons. Close the bathroom door next time ... By the way, what was the outcome of the brush with Marvin?"

"I chopped him."

"Er ... chopped?"

"Yes. It's a Japanese trick. We have a Japanese gym teacher ... She married a G.I. and has been here ten years. She showed us a lot of tricks to use on anxious men. She said it is called *karate*. She's good. She can split a pine plank and never hurt her hand."

Judge Cross looked above but seeing no light dropped his gaze to the girl again.

"Where did you chop him?"

"I chopped him twice. Once ..." She executed a lightning horizontal blow with the back of her left hand. "Like that across the solar plexus. When he bent over I…" She performed a vertical chopping motion. "… got him just behind the jaw."

The judge was irritated to find that he had been holding his breath. "That, I take it, was enough."

She nodded and sat down. "It was enough."

"Are you very athletic?"

"I suppose so. I love it. I play basketball, tennis, and Miss O'Brien… that's the Japanese teacher… she taught me *kendo*."

"What's that?"

"Japanese fencing. Then we took regular fencing. She wanted to learn how to use the saber, the foil and the epee. I'm strong and I fight back at her."

"Ummm, well, I guess we've talked enough for today." He sighed and looked at her. "My dear, I'm afraid you're a rebel. I'm not going to tell you what to do. You wouldn't do it. I'm afraid you are in a pretty bad spot, but it is not a spot that I can do anything about. Your father's legal position is not to be punctured unless by some overt act. All I can tell you is to go home, try to do the best you can under the circumstances. Try to keep down friction. In other words, try to get along with your step-father."

She was silent for a moment, then she smiled. "You know. I'd like to have you for a father."

"Me… why?"

"You're nice. You don't have a card index for a mind… I wouldn't fit, would I?"

"No, my dear, you wouldn't fit any ready-made index I ever saw."

"And yet you've been kind… I know I make people uncomfortable sometimes. Maybe I even like to. You've done your best. You didn't swallow Archie's tale like a catfish. You realize that I have a side in this argument." She smiled wider until a dimple showed in her right cheek. "You know, I think you'd even be a little on my side if you could."

He nodded soberly. "Yes, I would. In fact, I'm afraid I am. That, of course, you must keep confidential. It wouldn't do for it to be breathed about that Judge Cross plays favorites."

She nodded in turn. "I know ... But you know, don't you, that you've said what you had to say but that it won't work?"

"It won't?"

"No sir. You don't quite appreciate what sort of man Archie is. If he was a generous-hearted dog, that'd ogle me shamelessly and maybe pinch me on the behind occasionally, then I'd be willing to say he had ideas and that'd probably be the end of it. It isn't that way. My mother said she never inflamed a man in her life like she did Archie. I'm afraid, sir, that I do, too." She stood up and smoothed her hands slowly over her body from breasts to hips. "I'm afraid I have that rape shape Mamma predicted."

Judge Cross got out his handkerchief and mopped his balding brow. "I don't think there's any doubt about it. Now, I shall terminate this interview. Watch the er, shape, and keep it under wraps, as it were. Now just one more thing. If things get bad, if you feel that you can't handle any given situation, then do not hesitate to call me. If you just want to talk, remember the old man and come see me." He looked at her wistfully a moment, the vision of his own daughter dead for three years, and felt the choke of grief. He stood up and took both her hands in his own. "Come see me anyhow ... any time I have a free hour I'll be glad to talk to you."

She came quite close to him and placed her hand on his top vest button. "You're nice," she said, her voice cream-rich, her eyes deeply serious, then before he could stop her she came closer and kissed him on the lips with gentleness that almost broke his heart. She turned and was gone.

Judge Cross, hard man, just man, legal stalwart and one of the best minds in the bar associations, sat down slowly, bent his head to the surface of the desk and let tears fall from his eyes. The girl reminded him of Judy, his dead daughter. Suppose he had died early and Judy had been left to the mercies of an idiot like … He sat up, blew his nose angrily, mopped his eyes, and punched a button on his desk.

"Yes sir," came the voice of his secretary.

"Send in Archibald Denny," he said in a voice that made her jump.

Archibald Denny would not have recognized the face that had watched his stepdaughter out of the chambers as the flinty visage that now faced him. In fact, it was even more forbidding than it had been during the initial interview.

"Sit down, Mr. Denny," said the Judge and Archibald sat with a thump. He clasped his hands nervously and waited.

The Judge, for effect, studied the paper before him for a moment, then raised baleful eyes to the uneasy Archibald.

"As you know, Mr. Denny, when and if indications dictate we do considerable investigation into matters of this sort. By that I mean when a man comes in with a complaint which is not obviously supported by the facts."

Cross allowed this to sink in, hoping Archibald would say something. He did. "Then I am to go home without the help of this court? This court which I and the other taxpayers support? I must go home and have a repetition of this … this … deliberate defiance … Me, her father?" He leaned across the table and pounded it with his fist. "I pay your salary, sir, and I will not sit idly by and have this happen. This woman is spawned of the devil and I do not propose to sit idly by and see her fall into his clutches. I will not rear my fine boy in such an atmosphere."

"Is that a fact?" said Judge Cross mildly. "And what do you propose to do about it?"

"I …" Archibald snapped his mouth shut and floundered for a moment. "That is why I brought her before you. That's what this court is for, or don't you believe in prophylaxis?"

"As I started to say," said the judge, ignoring the last outburst, "we have investigated you thoroughly. We have investigated the girl and do you know what we found?"

"Plenty, probably," said Archibald virtuously. "I can't watch her all the time, therefore, I'll not be surprised at anything you discovered. She's very likely loose. I've watched her cavorting shamelessly with men, flouncing her skirt and revealing what I consider entirely too much leg. She wears shorts that should land her in jail. Now there's something you should do. Pass a law making it a crime to wear the horrible things. Shocking, that's what they are. I don't see why they just don't go nude and be done with it."

"That question bears more examination," said Cross offensively. "What my investigation discovered may come as a shock to you, but aside from normal juvenile hijinks, the girl is loved throughout the neighborhood. I find that she is helpful, cheerful, generous, she adores children. The younger generation becomes almost incoherent when describing her, particularly the boys…"

"Naturally," sneered Archibald nastily.

"They describe her," continued the judge, holding onto his temper, "in many strange but usual ways as 'the most', 'ultimate', 'pink extravagance', 'well dug,' 'love churn' and a few more that escape me. They, on the other hand, describe you as a drip, a jerk, a snod-goblin… whatever that is. One even called you Mr. Snagnasty. I mention these things merely to show as graphically as possible the reactions I received and just how far apart they are. The older people… with the exception of a few of your lodge brethren or whatever that cult is you belong to, seem to think you're 'peculiar'. One woman doubted that you'd ever had a human impulse in your life. Most of them were a bit sad that the girl should be left in your questionable care." Cross leaned forward. "I hope I am beginning to make myself clear."

Denny was almost purple with rage. "I'm afraid you're not."

"All right. I'll give it to you in short sentences using monosyllables when I can. I smell a herring that hasn't been in the ocean since I was a boy. This court does not intend to become any man's household watch dog. You made a complaint… You said she had run off. After investigation … and it took very little time, it was revealed that she had not run off at all. She had gone to a skating rink that is a reputable neighborhood place of amusement, run by a man and his wife who have children of their own and are models of respectability. No complaint has ever reached this office regarding any shady activities or unsavory incidents. She had been gone all of an hour and you knew where she was going."

"I did not know," stormed Archibald, now nearly apoplectic.

"In that case, I suggest you sue your next door neighbor, Mrs. Wallace, for malice because she overheard the row. The girl said where she was going and you forbade it. On what grounds is not plain. After all, skating with a girl friend is hardly immoral. The point I'm getting to is this. If this court is approached again on any subject dealing with Shayne Bennett, then, by God, you'd better come armed to the eyeballs with some facts because I can promise you that before this court takes any action on your say-so, a full, complete and detailed investigation will be made. Now, that's all I have to say on the matter. Good day."

During the last few minutes, Archibald Denny had gone from purple to white several times. He stood up.

"Then," he said in a harsh, strained voice, "you leave me no alternative. I know that you so-called modems frown on corporal punishment, but I do not. Therefore, since you are disposed to be sarcastic and lend an ear to neighborhood vindictiveness, I shall take things into my own hands. The next time she opposes me, I shall thrash her … something I should have done long ago."

Judge Cross smiled … he allowed it to expand into a chuckle. "By the way, Denny, are you familiar with the word *karate?*"

"No. It sounds like some heathen word."

The chuckle grew into a low laugh. "It is, Denny. Good day."

CHAPTER FIVE

"Let's be friends," said Marvin in a low voice as he sat on the couch beside Shayne.

"Why?" she asked.

He twitched and gripped his hands between his knees. "Well, isn't it the sort of things that people should do when under the same roof?"

"Maybe. Personally, I'd rather you went your way and I'll go mine."

"But you go days without even speaking to me."

"Let Annie B. rub your hurts," she snapped nastily.

"I don't like Annie B. all that much."

"That's not the way it came to me."

Marvin, ever since that day when he had seen her naked in the bathroom, had become increasingly aware that Shayne Bennett was something he was not likely to see equaled anywhere. Such girls as he had known were left far behind and now he had a nervous itch to possess her. Marvin, true to his total disregard of anything that did not directly relate to himself, had had some early and enlightening association with certain girls in high school who liked his clean-cut good looks, his fastidious dress and the mystery in his dark eyes. They had rendered unto Caesar the things that were his and that meant all.

When it first happened, his reactions were pointed and objective. He's been missing something, something he told himself he'd never miss again if he could possibly help it. Every time he saw Shayne he was missing something. He grew so absorbed with the idea that he even passed up other opportunities, something he had vowed never to do.

The fact that Shayne had stood before him as nude as a wiener was not, as he mistakenly thought, an invitation to greater things. His desire for her was continually at war with his desire for vengeance. It was true, she had never taken the tale of his downfall to school where he might well have been mortified to extinction had she done so, but the rankle was something that nagged him constantly … A girl, smashing him into dazed futility with her bare hands. That Shayne was powerful for a girl he was well aware, aside from personal experience. The boys in their horseplay didn't manhandle her. In tennis they went down to defeat with such regularity that she was always looking for a new partner. She had even enticed him to the courts once and had given him a sound drubbing. Her careless comment on the game was salt in his wounds.

"You didn't even make me sweat. Where'd you learn to play tennis … on a ping pong table?"

He was actually afraid of her. He had never been whipped by his parents and the only human who had ever humiliated him physically was Shayne.

It hurt him sorely to say it but he got it out. "If you'll go out with me, I won't look at another girl."

This sounded interesting, she had to admit, and she looked at him in surprise.

"That's a fact," he said, modulating his voice carefully.

"Maybe," she said with a casual air.

"Maybe what?" he asked.

"Maybe it's a fact. I don't know. I don't care." She got up and left him there, hating her and wanting her … knowing that if the hate made its appearance he'd not likely succeed in his want. Later that day he stole five dollars from a cache of his father's, thought to be secret. He bought her a small bottle of perfume which without his knowing she had wanted for a long time. It was an exciting grown-up scent that had once been presented to her mother. Marian hadn't thought it suited to her personality so she had allowed Shayne to play with it and waste most of it. Shayne, upon receiving the gift, was touched and Marvin went up in her estimation … so much so that she even decided that he wasn't such a bad egg after all. She even considered what it would be like to date him.

Shayne was orthodox in her tastes, and not too loyal to any one boy of her acquaintance. After one unpleasant experience with steady dating, she forsook the questionable security of the state and played the field. With her attractiveness she could afford to because she always had more boys at her beck and call than she needed. In fact, she was not greatly addicted to men at the time, still cherishing fast female friendships and often preferring their company. She did not have the proper attitude toward the boys because she was the physical superior of many of them and lacked the proper respect for the male sex.

"Let's go get a soda," suggested Marvin when he sensed the change of climate.

"Sure," she said with a smile that made his heart thud dangerously. "Wait till I change shoes."

They had the soda. They chatted gaily about nothing. They had a fine time. Another head-on clash with Archibald found her with Marvin's unequivocal support and this further entrenched him.

Marvin, with an instinct that might have been expected in an older man, bided his time and piled up favorable points in every way his agile and inventive mind could devise. Shayne was frankly flattered and accented his adoration as something really fine and enjoyable. She even allowed him to kiss her one night after a movie and was considerably angered at herself when she found that the caress had turned her knees to water and her will to nothing. Her mouth came open as if by instinct and Marvin, sensing the raging buildup of charging blood, bore her backward on the couch and poured all his talents into a kiss such as she had never before experienced.

She was like a bird, high in cold electrically charged air, soaring, soaring... her lips supersensitive, her body as pliable as a sapling bending to his every whim. The touch of his assaulting tongue that entered her acquiescent mouth was a scalding lash of torrid sensation that further weakened her. She knew that his hand was on her right breast, that other intimacies were beginning. A door slammed in the back and Marvin leaped erect as though stung, heard his father coming and skipped nimbly through the living room door into his room and shut his door. When Archibald came into the living room, she still lay on the couch, her skirt around her waist, the length of her tanned legs glimmering in the dim overhead light. For a second he stood stricken at the sight, noting as he watched that she was blinded by some overwhelming passion. She was her mother's daughter... that was it. She was like her mother, even more beautiful, in the rare tenderness of early womanhood.

Archibald, ever a man to deny his animal heritage, was at the same time a babe in its grasp and with a moan of mingled anguish and desire, he fell to his knees.

Shayne, still numb from the impact of the first storm of passion she had ever experienced, scarcely knew who he was or if she did the knowledge could not fight past the viscid red flood that had engulfed her. She knew that she was being handled, that the handling was deepening the state of inaction that held her in its grip. She knew when her last protection was stripped from her and when the sensation struck that made the rest seem as nothing.

Her body stung now from its static inaction, in a tempo as old as humanity and everything went black for a few seconds, relieving her in its cataclysmic wonder from the tensions and confusion... and what she saw horrified her beyond measure.

With an exclamation of furious disgust she smashed her feet with all her strength into Archibald's face. He went backward, fell hard and his head struck the piano stool. She got up, ill, trembling, torn from a fury of emotions for which she was not prepared, appalled at the experience she had gone through, filled with nauseous revolt from the memory of the man's utter loss of control and his subsequent act. She stood and looked down at him, shaking as though in the throes of a violent chill.

Marvin took her by the arm. "You did just right," he said gently. "Now why don't you go to bed?"

She let him lead her to her room where as soon as she heard the door close behind him, she fell across her bed and went through a stormier spell of weeping than she could remember. Later, her body and mind drained dry and purged somewhat by the relief of weeping, she got up and sneaked quietly into the bathroom where she scrubbed herself sore in a tub of hot water until she had washed away every vestige of his touch.

Her recovery was rapid and before she left the bathroom she had admired herself in the long mirror, speculated over the power she seemed to have over men, shuddered again at the memory, was thankful that the shudder was less than it might have been and that after all she had not been physically injured. Upon the heels of healing spirit came thoughts more acceptable but no less related to the night's occurrence. What had come over her? Why had the kiss done that to her?

Of one thing she was sure. The kiss alone hadn't done it. It had been a combination of kiss, the effects of Marvin's hands... but how had Archibald come into the picture? She hadn't recalled him being anywhere around. Dear, dear Marvin. He had been so thoughtful. She had done just right, he said. She hugged her breasts, acutely conscious of them now. They were so sensitive that she almost cried out. She dropped her hands down her flanks and stroked her smooth hips. There were other thoughts that came then. There were, she had discovered, a great many things about herself that she had not suspected.

She went to bed then but it was a long time before sleep came to her.

In the living room Marvin waited until his father groaned and sat up. He sat on the couch and watched the older man come by degrees to his senses.

"I've seen a good many things in my life," said Marvin, managing to sound like a much-travelled man, "but this I never saw before. What do you suppose Judge Cross would think if he knew?"

Archibald, stricken with the memory of his act, tottered to his feet, and almost fell into a chair.

"My cross is too heavy to bear," he moaned.

"I should think it would be."

"You saw ...?"

"I saw and I must say I wouldn't have believed it. And you a grown-up."

Archibald's eyes were stricken and getting to his feet, he staggered back to his bedroom where he flung himself across the bed and prayed wildly, incoherently ... then fell into an exhausted sleep:

Marvin had waited for some time and he could afford to wait longer. It would, he felt, not be too long.

Waiting proved to be his undoing, however, and Annie B. who had chafed under being ignored, renewed her attentions to the point where Marvin capitulated. Moreover, having even more contempt for her than usual, he ignored one of the safety tenets of a successful cavalier and Annie B. became with child. Marvin panicked and without even telling anyone what he was contemplating, he joined the Navy and left town. There was considerable stir and scandal which Archibald fought with dogged tenacity and finally got the heat removed when a private detective he had hired discovered that Annie B. was most profligate with her affections and even in her early pregnancy was still in high demand as a date.

Shayne, sickened by the whole thing, was relieved when she discovered that Marvin had finally fallen prey to his vast pride. He could not conceive of anyone making headway with Annie B., when she might have had him so he was forced to accept responsibility for an act that might not have been his fault after all.

After his last fall, Archibald seemed to retire within his shell and to Shayne's surprise took to drink. She wondered what mental gymnastics he had performed to make it right with himself. Something quite complicated and to him reasonable, no doubt. He took to staying away from home for long periods which suited her to perfection.

She entered the university business school and paid for it with the money left by her mother. She bought and paid for what groceries she used, taking most of her meals out. She studied hard, made good grades and had almost no social life, although she was constantly harried by importunate males.

As she matured she found a peace of mind which was reflected in her face and body. While she'd play hard grinding tennis and fence like a demon, making more than one instructor wonder why he had ever bothered to take up the sport, she managed to avoid male entanglements. She had no objection to men, in fact there were times when her self-imposed singularity irked her sorely, but something always made her keep them at arm's length.

CHAPTER SIX

At the age of nineteen, Shayne Bennett was a beauty that made men stop and stare. She was conscious of it and very likely dressed and acted to attract them, but none managed to crack the defense with which she had surrounded herself.

In a manner known only to himself, Judge Cross now retired—heard about it. He had never forgotten her and every time he thought of her, he'd think of his dead daughter. He pondered for days over the impulse he had to talk to her, examined his motives until he was thoroughly confused, then in a sort of despair he called her anyway.

"I want to talk to you," he said frankly, having decided that with Shayne, frankness was the only possible policy.

"It was sweet of you to think of me, sir," she said in a throaty, affectionate voice. "I've thought of you many times and I've wanted to talk to you, too."

"When shall it be?"

"This afternoon?"

"Well ... no. I have a few cases that I'll have to attend to this afternoon."

"Tomorrow?"

"Why yes, that would be fine. Tomorrow it is ... Oh dear ..."

"What's the matter?"

"Oh, the devil. I told my caretaker I'd come out to the camp tomorrow and see about some repairs he thinks are needed. I can't tell him to wait because I don't have a phone out there ..."

"I'd love to see your camp. Suppose I drive out right after noon and we can have a long talk?"

"That would be bully," he said. "Make it at noon and I'll have some fish fixed that will melt in your mouth."

"That's a date ... Bye."

After a fine dinner of Amite River catfish, hot cornbread and a tangy, tossed salad, they went to the front porch that overlooked the river and sat in deep chairs.

"I like it here," she said comfortably. "Complete privacy, quiet ..."

"I know," he said somberly. "It's my retreat. I come here to do my deepest pondering. What's with you?"

She turned and smiled. "What did you want to talk about?"

He fidgeted. "I'm not sure I wanted to talk about anything. Maybe I'm just an old man who has seen so many rents and seams in the garment of life that I just have a longing to look at something that is clean, undefiled, unbelievably lovely ..." He smiled. "Lord, If I could lose forty years would I ever give you a chase. What's this business about you causing a minor upheaval every time you walk across the campus and yet you never even allow a man a chance to state his case?"

She was silent for a while looking at the clear water that gurgled past. A white egret poised with delicate grace in the shallow water intent upon a minnow. A kingfisher fell with a noisy splash into the water and filched the minnow from beneath the egret's nose.

"That's hard to answer, Judge. If I were to say that I'm not interested in men, I'd be lying. There's just some little something that makes me turn them down. It could be related to a little unpleasantness I had a couple of years ago." Simply and without heat she told him euphemizing some of the more unpleasant details.

"Why didn't you come to see me?" he asked, forcing gentleness into his voice, his face red with anger.

"I don't know. I thought about it at the time."

"Are you in love with Marvin?"

"We write and I'm fond of him. He made quite a change after that first trouble when Archie went to the police. I'm not sure why I didn't yell for help but I didn't. Is it possible that I..." She hesitated fractionally. "Maybe the fact that when all was said and done, the experience, in spite of having been a rotten, sordid sort of thing, was enjoyed subconsciously... Maybe I didn't take the attitude of spoiled womanhood because deep down I didn't feel spoiled or soiled. Now what does that make me?"

He sighed. "I'd say that what you've just told me makes you one of the strongest personalities I ever encountered. Haven't you heard of compensation, of the sorry efforts people make to confront themselves with a fact? Haven't you ever wanted to dress a situation up so that you'd come out with colors flying? Haven't you ever wanted to juggle the facts so as to show you in a better light?"

"I suppose so, but I don't feel that I have to pose or strut for you. If I expect what you say to do me any good. then you need to have all the facts. Not as I might dress them up but as they are. People seem to get over the awfullest calamities. I suppose that, in truth, the calamities aren't so bad after all. The question is always to me. is it as bad as you first thought? The answer is usually, no. I think that public knowledge of what had happened to me would have hurt me more than the fact itself."

"You're just not so," he said. "I had the most peculiar feeling when I called you that I'd wish I hadn't. Do you know that I'm always just a little aghast at your bluntness, your simplicity, the seeming indifference to compensatory protection? I can see the value of your attitude but where did you get it? How?"

"From my mother, I suppose. The longer she's dead, the more I can see what a wonderful person she was. I think she was a great deal like me. Dad, my real one, not Archibald, always said that he gave up trying to understand her early. After that he just tagged along and liked it." She twisted around in her chair. "Do you think maybe I'm like I am because of some ingrained desire to be different, to be a rebel, to fight against conformity … if Joanne Blow is this or that way, then I'll be damned if I'll be?"

He nodded. "We couldn't say for sure because we don't yet know how or why the human mind reacts as it does. All I know is that you're probably the loveliest woman I ever saw. You are also seemingly the simplest, most direct, least complicated person I know. Everything is either black or white to you. You aren't sure of everything, true, but you're pretty certain about that. You had a terrible experience, a shock, and yet the way you tell it, most of the effect had disappeared by morning."

"I think it had. In a week's time what I was mostly concerned with was my own reaction to something new."

"You needn't answer this, but have you ever tried to seek it again … expose yourself to a man?"

"I don't mind answering. I've thought about it a million times. I've been loved to distraction in day-dreams, right down to the last detail, but not in fact. Maybe I don't let men come to see me because of that fear. Maybe under pressure I'd wilt again."

"I doubt that it would ever creep up on you again like that. I think you're forewarned now."

"I'm not sure. I wish I could be. You see. I'm a person who doesn't know social life as other girls do. It must be a fear that something in me is ready, waiting to be touched off."

He nodded. "That could be, but where will it end?"

"I don't know. Marvin gets out of the Navy soon and I'll see him, of course. Maybe I'll use him as a test."

He shifted uneasily. "You know, I don't like that lad. Something about him makes me uneasy."

She laughed and slid her chair close to his and put a hand over his. "You're in love with me yourself and you're jealous."

He nodded, grinning. "That's probably correct … the louse. What does he mean wanting my Shayne … Shayne … Your name is as lovely as you are."

She stood up and looked down at him, almost overcome by a rush of affection. "Judge, do you have a blanket?"

"Couple on the bed in the back room ... why?"

"Oh ... just an idea I have. It struck me all of a sudden." She disappeared into the camp and was gone five minutes.

He watched the water roll by as inexorable as time. Judge Cross was resenting his age as he often did when he thought of Shayne. What was she up to now? Whatever it was, he wouldn't be prepared for it. Of that he was certain. A blanket ... What on earth did she want with a blanket on a spring day like this?

She came un and walked to the edge of the porch and turned. She was muffled to the chin in an old army blanket.

"You have said that I'm beautiful. You said it in a kind way without leering or winking. You are a generous, unselfish, wonderful, gentleman. I think you worship beauty ... just as something that is the most important thing in the world to you. Just this once ... just because I love you dearly, I want you to see how beautiful I really am."

She loosed the blanket and let it slide slowly to her feet, standing in its center, straight, tall, proud, a sight that time would never be able to erase.

Judge Cross thought of himself as an old man, although he was only sixty. This, he felt certain, was the last time he would ever see such a sight nor could he ever remember having seen anything like it in the past. Without a single string of a garment, she stood before him, her eyes calm, her face untouched by the blush of shame ... Shame, he threw the word from his mind as he would have thrown a hot pebble from his hand. It sounded, even unuttered, like blasphemy. To be ashamed of a body like Shayne Bennett's would be to curse God's handiwork and certainly she had every reason to be proud of it. From her shapely feet to the crown of her sun-tawny hair she was the most poetic creation he had ever seen.

He remembered his previous thoughts about exaggeration. It was less apparent now that she was without clothes. If such there was it was so well proportioned to the whole that there was no sign of it now. Her thighs, stomach, the vain cliffs of her solid breasts with their rosebud tips ... the entire expanse of her body shone with an inner incandescence, a flame that mere proto-plasm could only dim but never obscure, sheened on the surface with the dull glow of nature's ripe, nourishing oils, a portrait to passion, to love, to beauty that beggared description.

"It's like being made love to," she whispered, "just watching your face. You wouldn't know what it's like being a woman and seeing what she can do to a man ... at a distance ... without con-tact, without even a suggestion of impropriety ... just apprecia-tion. Am I wrong in knowing that I'm beautiful and loving it?"

"No." he said in a choked voice. "I think the worst thing in the world that could happen to you would be *not* knowing it. What the future holds for you unless some tragedy happens and if something did happen what a tragedy it *would* be! Helen, not-withstanding her thousand ships, was a washwoman." He stood up, clenching his hands to stop them from shaking, then opened them to place them on her shoulders. The shock was almost more than he could stand.

"Do just one more thing for the old man," he begged.

Her smile was the illumination of innocence. "I will, of course. I'm not afraid of anything that you might ask."

"Go whack that diving board yonder with your feet and dive into the river. It's very deep there. Swim around a while. I've seen it standing still. Now I want to see it in motion,"

Her white even teeth flashed, she whirled and ran down the long steps to the wharf, bounding springily along like a doe. She ran to the diving board, gave a lithe spring, struck the end of the board and rose upward like a bird, her arms back, her hair fly-ing, her body in a fabulous arch. At the height of the spring she curved forward, to his fascinated eyes like slow motion, and went down. Her arms whipped around in a quick arc and she entered the water arrow-straight. So perfectly did she execute the dive that her body entered the water with a soft, almost splashless, plop.

For five minutes she split the water with effortless strokes, rolling and diving like a dolphin slipping through the water with all the grace and ease of that active fish. She rolled over on her back and floated for a moment, then began a slow backdive that was the climax of her efforts. So slowly did she perform it that Judge Cross held his breath in speechless wonder. Her breasts, water-hard and spiked like new buds slowly disappeared from the surface, then the water climbed her stomach, then further until her golden middle submerged to be followed by the marble-smooth columns of her thighs. The judge sat shakily on a piling and watched as she burst from the depths like a mermaid. Her face alight with pleasure, her teeth gleaming in the sunlight.

"Getting cold," she yelled. "Got a towel?"

He nodded and mounted the steps to the camp where he found a thick, white, terry cloth robe and brought it to her. She reached up for a hand, grasped it, placed her feet on the little wharf and bounded out of the water in one lithe spring. She stood for a moment on the planking, letting the water cascade from her body in crystalline drops, others standing on her tanned skin and glinting like sapphires in the sun. Then she put on the robe and hugged it to her all over, letting the absorbent cloth take up the water. She tied the sash and caught him by the arm. "I'll let you fix me a big highball while I dress."

When they got to the porch she saw that he had brought her clothes to the porch and a little throb went through her heart. Why hadn't she known this wonderful man all her life? Why hadn't she seen more of him once she had found him? There was something wildly exciting exposing her ripe nudity to his frankly appreciative gaze, something holy in the stark admiration in his eyes, untainted with even a suggestion of lechery... and yet she knew that desire had touched him. She admired him because of the fact that he, in spite of being a man, could look and not become lost, could savor to the utmost the priceless picture of her body in all its pristine wonder. He started into the camp to fix the drink but she stopped him.

"If you wanted to see me dress, the drink can wait." The judge stopped and sat heavily in a chair, grateful for the fact that the hot blood that should have risen to his face stayed in its normal channels. He *had* wanted to see her dress and had brought the clothes out on the porch for that reason.

She took a pair of breezily frilled white briefs from the pile of clothing and shucking out of the robe slipped them on with a single smooth effort. She then sat and drawing up one still damp thigh she drew on a sock. The other followed, then she put on a plaid shirt ... no bra, he noticed, and swallowed drily as he did, then her light grey woolen skirt. Her shoes followed, then she sat back with a sigh.

"Now, I'd like that drink."

He brought it and wondered at the inaction of his tongue, he, a man whose acid phrases had rolled sonorously and often from his judicial lips. Now he was dumb.

She buried her nose in the frosty highball and smiled at him over the top of it.

"This has been a wonderful day," she murmured. "What some people wouldn't think of me for what I did ..." She shivered a little. "And I got the biggest bang out of it I ever had."

"I," he said positively, "got such a bang out of it that for a while I was not sure I'd survive."

"I know," she said softly. "I saw it in your eyes ... I could read your mind and I didn't dislike a thing I read."

"Make me a promise," he said as he held his lighter for her cigarette. "Come see me. Don't wait so long next time."

"I won't. That's a promise. Now I think I'd better get along. Marvin just might come in this afternoon and I'm anxious to see him."

"Why?"

"I don't know, really. I think it's because I sort of want to test me. I'm not certain what it is. It seems that meeting him will settle something in my mind. I might like what I see and I might not."

"May I ask a personal question?"

"Of course."

"Will you let him take you?"

She frowned and dragged hard on the cigarette. "I don't know...truthfully. He could have that time. I couldn't have raised a finger. Maybe that's part of a test. I just don't know."

"Well, let me know how everything comes out. I'm interested, you know."

"I know," she replied, her eyes as soft as pansies. She sat on the arm of his chair and kissed him with a sweetness that made his heart ache wildly. "Now I must go. I'll see you soon and tell you everything."

He laughed a little erratically. "That's just it. You say you'll tell me everything. You'll do it, too."

For a long time after she left, Judge William Acabaeus Cross sat in his chair and stared at the hypnotic flow of the river and listened to the silences of the pines and oaks.

The sun was shining brightly but her leaving had been like the throwing of a switch...the light having dimmed. Sourly, he stood up and stretched, thinking that he had a drink coming and that a drink was a poor substitute for Shayne.

CHAPTER SEVEN

Charles Corbett Carraway, the Third, found out in less than a week that an idle mind is the devil's workshop. Lavender had been ushered from the house without protest but anyone could see that she simmered at a high heat...if futilely. With the evidence that he had against her, her lips were effectively sealed. With the legal aspects of the separation over, Charles found time a deadly anchor on his hands. He golfed, went fishing, took a trip to New York and saw all the shows, went to seven baseball games and none of these things drew any more enthusiasm from him than might be covered by a lazy yawn.

He tried to interest himself in giving parties for plant officials and technical men but since he had never enjoyed them, he wondered why he had given them.

Dr. Carmicheal collared him at the finish of a party one night and gave him a talk.

"What'n hell's wrong with you, boy? You look like a last year's bird nest."

Charles shrugged. "No interest, Doctor. Too much time on my hands."

The doctor snorted. "That's a hell of an excuse. Why don't you have fun?"

"I guess it was conditioned out of me. I've thought and thought but I don't seem to have any interests."

"What's wrong with an interest in the gals. They condition that out of you, too?"

Charles smiled thinly. "No, I guess not but for some reason I could never be very casual about that. It's got to mean something more than … than …"

"Than a biological collision?"

"Yes. I guess that's about the size of it. I have no moral scruples about it, but …" He shrugged.

"Well, what's wrong with travel? Surely they didn't condition general interest out of you. See new places, do new things. Look the gals over. Maybe one'll pop up who'll untie that knot."

Charles nodded. "And tie another one? No thanks, I've had all the legal entanglements I want with woman."

"It doesn't take but one of the right sort to shred the pants off that resolution." The doctor got up. "Why'n the devil don't you find some sort of woodsy retreat … a cabin in the pines or sumpn. Get away from all these people that make you retch. Get by yourself … get lost. Just one thing, though, boy, go south. It takes more guts to last one of these winters out than it does to rive out fifty thousand cedar shingles. I might take it into my head to join you and if I do I want it to be somewhere in a sunny clime. Tell you what. Go to Louisiana … Baton Rouge, to be explicit, and look up Dan Woodward. He's with Esso down there but they don't get much work out of him. He spends most of his time in the woods and on the streams hunting and fishing. Talk to him and let him make suggestions. I'm being vague but so are your complaints."

Charles thought it over and with a few changes followed the advice. He had always loved flying so he bought a four-place Cessna and took off with a vague idea that he'd explore the south. He ran out of United States quicker than he had any idea he would and found himself in Houston with no place to go but east or west. He decided on east and ignoring the airport manager's advice that he dog-leg the worst of the swamp area so that he might be able to glide to a safe forced landing, if such became necessary, took off holding a compass course for Baton Rouge.

He also neglected to file a flight plan, something the manager might have advised, but was too intent on telling him about the dangers of the swamp, in the event of a forced landing.

Charles should not have been flying. Given to wool gathering when thinking about something else he was flying by instinct, and the quality of his instinct was wanting. His longing for Edna was an occupation which occupied most of his waking hours.

He passed over Lake Charles ... he passed over Crowley and he passed over Lafayette. The first inkling he had that he had a fuel problem did not come from his gauges. He hadn't so much as glanced at them.

His motor gave a few warning coughs and snapped him out of his reverie. He switched tanks and heard the motor catch and purr smoothly. Then, belatedly, he tried to find himself.

He studied his map, remembered vaguely having passed over a fairly large town, tried to ferret out the identity of it and failed. Still he had his compass and by continuing due east he was sure to sight the Mississippi River. If, he told himself, the weather holds ...

He glanced behind him and caught a splash of red marking the sunset. Ahead the story was different. There was an ominous blackness building up from the far north to the far south. He was approaching a front. The logical thing was for him to return to the last town he had seen, but he began an argument with himself that was to do him ill. What if he failed to locate the town ...? dark was coming swiftly and he only had part of one tank of fuel. According to his calculations, he was only forty or fifty miles from the Mississippi. Unless the weather ahead was really vile he should be able to get under it and reach New Orleans or Baton Rouge.

He shifted course so as to line up for the capital of Louisiana and opened the throttle until his airspeed indicator was holding on one-hundred and fifty miles per hour. He eased off when he remembered that he was using fuel too fast and at that moment he struck the first gust.

Below him was a black, forbidding stretch as far as the eye could reach, but out of the blackness swam a thin ribbon of silver. The Mississippi? His heart gave a glad leap but one glance at the map showed him he was wrong.

It was the Atchafalaya.

His throat grew taut for a moment but he felt better when he realized he was quite close to Baton Rouge. Only about forty or fifty miles.

Before the feeling of safety could take hold, he felt his craft in the grip of a tremendous updraft.

For a long moment he fought the sturdy plane as it flipped and spun at the mercy of the furious wind. Shrieking air currents made him slam his throttle nearly shut, fearing that he might pull a wing off.

Luckily he had not removed his safety belt but loosened it after takeoff, else he might have been tossed against the overhead and stunned.

Suddenly he came out of the current and was astounded to see that he had seven-thousand feet of altitude.

Lightning began to flash and grew brasher and more lurid as he bored into the heart of the storm. Rain began to lash at him with a fury he had never encountered before. An avalanche of hail struck the plane and the crash almost stopped his heart. One stone larger than the rest caught the tip of his propeller and damaged it enough to set up a dangerous vibration.

He throttled back again until the vibration diminished. Looking at his altimeter, he saw that the maximum R.P.M.'s he could maintain and not cause vibrational damage was below that required to keep him airborne.

Sweat broke out on his forehead as he realized that he could not remain airborne for more than ten minutes at the most. Moreover, he was now lying southwest.... something he had not immediately noticed when he came out of the updraft, being fully occupied by other considerations.

He corrected his course and watched the altimeter needle unwind with clock-like slowness. The rain thinned but now he was in something worse. Fog had rolled in from the Gulf and now he was flying in a wooly ball of soupy air so thick he could not even see his propeller. He turned on his landing lights and tried to raise Ryan Airport in Baton Rouge on his radio. He managed to collect a notable spray of rasping crackling static but after repeated calls and no answer, he kept repeating the story of his predicament.

"Going down in Atchafalaya swamp. Think I'm east of Atchafalaya River. Not certain. Prop damaged. Can't remain airborne over five more minutes. Altitude fifteen-hundred feet."

The landing lights exploded into a cottony ball of frustration against the impenetrable fog but Charles left them on. He might come to a rift, maybe get under it. If he did he might have a chance to pick some little spot not as bad as if he had to go in blind.

He tightened his belt until it cut into his stomach and put his fingertips on his switches. If he had a chance, he'd cut the switches just before he struck and lessen the danger of fire. He glanced at the fuel gauge. Not enough gas left to make a good fire, he thought.

A mass of rain-wet green, swam into view with the speed of a bullet and he hauled back on the wheel, felt the plane shudder as it thrashed through the top of a tall cypress.

His face tense, drenched with sweat, white and set, he leaned forward and tried to force his vision through the fog. He glanced swiftly at the altimeter and it was registering forty feet. He might be anywhere from ground level to sixty feet.

Suddenly, the landing light seemed to leap through the fog which had thinned. Below him was a long, straight stretch of water some eighty feet wide and as calm as glass.

With a sob of relief, he dropped his flaps, cut throttle and switches. Down, down he went until at last he heard what he thought was his wheels cutting a thin wave in the water, then he hauled back with all his might.

The nose came up briefly, then settled back, the wheels dug in and the plane soughed into the water and did a neat flip coming to rest upside down. This last Charles did not know. He now hung upside down in his safety belt, a knot rapidly rising over his temple.

CHAPTER EIGHT

From the spillway levee at Ramah, Louisiana, to the Atchafalaya River is a forbidding stretch that to measure in miles would be of little meaning unless one were to fly over it. To a man afoot it is an invitation to death. In a small boat, a test that only the strong may pass. It is a morass of mud and a jungle of tupelo gum, saw-toothed palmetto, buckvine, water hyacinth, over-cup oak, cypress and buttonwood swamps as tough and impenetrable as mangroves. It is a labyrinth of slowly meandering bayous flowing with black water … black from decaying vegetable matter, but clear in the sense that no mud is present in the water unless during flood times or the mud flow from numerous oil wells that dot the swamp area.

The sun was setting in a sullen blood bath sending back searching fingers of scarlet trimmed in lead, fingers that reached far back into the east to caress the frowning anvils of thunderheads the bases of which were alive with summer lightning.

Uncle Henry Pelichet stood in his houseboat door at the mouth of King's Ditch, an old float road and drain that had seen hundreds of thousands of feet of cypress timber float out of the swamp into the borrow pit to be rafted and towed to the mill in Plaquemine.

Uncle Henry shifted his weight to his good leg, hitched his artificial limb over the jamb of the doorway and finally settled on the tiny porch of the houseboat. He fumbled with work-hardened hands, found his pipe, stuffed it with Redtag, cut-plug, gripped it precariously between his gums and lighted it.

He turned keen brown eyes toward the flaming horizon, removed his hat and ran his fingers absently through his hair. His sharp-hard visage looked Indian in the false rosy light. He spat irritably into the glassy-brown water and watched the splash where a gar had broken the surface for his infrequent gasp of air.

Uncle Henry fidgeted uneasily. Something was in the air and he couldn't pinpoint it. He disliked premonitions because though he rarely had a false one, the thing had to happen before he could identify it. His stump prickled and the air was too quiet. The borrow pit too unruffled, the sky too red and ominous looking, and his son Danny too unconcerned.

Danny, a powerful light ginger colored man weighing some two-hundred and fifteen pounds with his six feet of height was too modern to have premonitions and too sensible to ignore those of his father's. At the moment Danny was recuperating from a hard day's fishing and was stretched on the couch inside the houseboat snoring wholeheartedly.

"Get up from there," growled his father, "and go get me some beer at the Chute."

Danny grunted, smacked his lips, blew like a grampus and resumed his snoring.

Uncle Henry grimaced and got up. Carefully he lowered himself into a *pirogue* and paddled with professional strokes southward where the Chute rested on topped cypress trees, five feet above flood stage and provided fishermen and trappers with beer, cheap wine and whiskey.

Patty-U Bend was two miles south but two miles was hardly enough to put sweat on Uncle Henry's forehead so he stopped the boat at the wharf at the foot of the long stairway, still unwinded. He tied the painter with an expert twitch of his wrist. Slowly and with care he climbed to the rickety wharf.

"This thing is gonna drown somebody one day," he grumbled.

Uncle Henry made his way up the steps, opened the gesture of a screen door and walked into the dimly lit interior. He doffed his hat politely and spoke to all present. The proprietor first, as was his custom.

"Mr. Ponce ... Mr. Elf ... Mr. Bob ... Miss Bertha ... Mr. Jim ... Miss Aggy ... Miss Phoney."

Uncle Henry stopped and might have been seen to blush. Miss Phoney always did make him uncomfortable because she always seemed to be in the process of embarrassing her husband, wizened and bleary-eyed Fletch Unger. Moreover, she responded to greetings about one time in ten and few people but Uncle Henry ever bothered to speak to her.

At the moment she was chewing on Fletch's right ear and Fletch was weeping into his muscatel. He was hardly an attractive man, his face having caved in from the loss of his teeth and his mouth seemed permanently shriveled and lined, puckering inward to a tiny aperture which opened most often to admit a draught of port, muscatel or sherry. The others spoke with varying degrees of cordiality because most of them respected Uncle Henry for his quiet dignity, something they lacked in various degrees, a matter for which some of them secretly hated the old colored man.

Uncle Henry walked sedately to the splintery cypress bar stained and scarred by brawls and careless drinking.

Uncle Henry looked at the owner, Mr. Ponce Unger, brother of Mr. Fletch, with an uncertain grin.

"Even', Mr. Ponce," he said again.

"Evenin' Henry." Ponce Unger was slat thin and rail tall, scant of chin and prominent of brow, giving him the appearance of a bird of prey about to pounce. His nose, an appendage that might have contained life of its own, helped the impression.

"Six cans of Baltz beer, Mr. Ponce. In a bag."

"Sure, Henry..." Mr. Ponce bent over to dip the beer out of half a barrel filled with water and ice. Mr. Ponce, having sampled his own wares assiduously lost his balance and went headfirst up to his shoulders in the icy water. He caught the sides of the barrel and emerged blowing and snorting.

"Dag nab the dag nabbed so and so, the son of this, that and the other ... lef' mud on my floor. Might drown a man."

Uncle Henry nodded with alacrity, trying to smother the mirth that rose in his chest. "That's the truth, Mr. Ponce, that's the truth. Them careless people ought to slip on their own mud ... and break their own necks."

Mr. Ponce blew again, choking with indignation, shivered a little and wiped his face with a filthy bar rag.

"Dag nab it, Henry, you've got more hod-tasseled sense'n any ten swamp rats I know. Takes a man with some sense to grieve with a man. Have a beer on me."

"Yes, sir," said Uncle Henry, his mirth under control now. "Thank you, kindly. One for the trip would be fine."

Uncle Henry drank with slow dignity and Mr. Ponce compared him favorably to ... well, hell, his own brother, Fletch. Fletch had come in frothing for a drink and had downed a pint of muscatel before he even sat at a table. Fletch was no good. Uncle Henry was a gentleman who paid his bills.

Mr. Ponce eased out a dirty forefinger and touched Uncle Henry's elbow. "See them two?" He inclined his head toward his brother and Mrs. Euphonio Unger ... that's the way she appeared on the voting lists. "Regia' cootch cat, that Phoney ... and Fletch ... Won't stay offen the wine long enough t' give her a good ridin'. Think she suffers? Hunh unh, not her. The way she throws it around, somebody'll get 'er 'fore she gets back to Tweed's Pass. Look at that there Weezer Wagner. Skinnin' 'is eyeballs at 'er right now."

Uncle Henry was uncomfortable. He cast a sidelong glance at Weezer who stood at the other end of the bar casting heated glances at Miss Phoney who had ceased her attacks on Fletch's left ear and was looking back at Weezer, her enormous grey eyes as bold as a fighting cock's.

"Er ... Mr. Fletch don't never get his musk up?" asked Uncle Henry cautiously.

"He ain't got none," averred Mr. Ponce. "She wiggles it in his face ever' time she can get anybody t' look, like now... See what I mean?"

Miss Phoney had taken her eyes off Weezer and was doing things with Fletch's hand under the table. Uncle Henry turned his eyes away and began to study the fly-specked solunar table tacked on the wall behind the bar. Thunder muttered heavily in the east and a flicker of blue lightning gave the mean bar a cheap garish definition.

Miss Phoney, done with manipulating Fletch's hand along her silken thigh, reached over and seized the ear again between her strong white teeth. Fletch carefully elevated the bottle to his mouth, drank, then put it back on the table and began to weep again. Miss Phoney released him and sat back in her chair with a sensuous motion that made her breasts heave heavily about inside her threadbare cotton dress. She was proud of them and what they did to men and not without reason.

In fact, Euphonia Madrigal had, it seemed, come from quality folks but in some manner she had become attached to the swamp and Fletch Unger, and now bore his name by virtue of common law.

Miss Phoney was a woman who might arrest attention anywhere she was allowed to perform without restraint. She was large, she was tall, she had a certain primitive grace about her, and an indolent body-rolling walk that invited assault. Her face was petulantly lovely, her lips heavy, sensuous and uninhibited, her breasts high, firm and assertive, her waist narrow and her stomach plated with the long flat muscle of a belly dancer. Her hips flared richly and contributed no little to the seductive walk which never failed to set men's hearts to racing and their minds to plotting. She rarely wore shoes but her feet had not flattened and splayed like some of her swamp sisters. They were small well-formed and high arched, contributing to the slim ankles and the shapely, strong calves.

Weezer was still looking so Miss Phoney crossed her legs in a manner that made him blink. Never had he seen so much velvety skin on one woman.

Weezer's vision blurred a little and he became faint. He was not, by heart, the romantic type and most of his experience had been bought in various bordellos at the end of cane grinding season, the only time Weezer ever had any ready cash. He was a poor fisherman and an indifferent trapper so only during the sugar season did he feel that fun was more important than food. Weezer was not a romancer, mainly because he was six feet four inches tall, weighed a hundred and forty pounds, had a superb proboscis and a receding chin. Folks said that he looked too much like Ponce Unger for coincidence but nothing could be proven.

He heaved a ragged sigh but was then struck with a pang of hope as Fletch drained the last of his wine and fell face down on the table top, his mouth falling open and a little trickle of wine and saliva issuing forth.

"Passed out," thought Weezer triumphantly. He got up and ambled awkwardly over to the table. "Eve nin', Miss Phoney," he said in his high croaking voice. "Looks like you're needin' help."

Miss Phoney stretched her arms backward and leaned the chair back, stretching tremendously. The act thrust her breasts into such violent contact with her dress that Weezer held his breath wondering if they'd burst through. She relaxed with a thump then yawned widely.

"Yeah," she said throatily. "I could use some help. Le's get 'im to the boat."

Weezer, as frail as he appeared, handled Fletch with ease and Miss Phoney followed him closely, her right breast prodding him in the left shoulder.

"See what I mean?" said Ponce, darkly.

"Well…" Uncle Henry hastily drained his beer and picked up the bag containing more. "Thank you kindly for the beer," he said. "Looks like rain."

"Thunder 'fore seven, rain 'fore 'leven," quoted Ponce looking at his watch. "Dammit, I'm 'bout froze stiff. Bertha, go get me a fresh shirt."

"You ain't got none," said Bertha over seven empty beer cans. "That'n you got on is the las' one. Tole you a month ago to go get yourself a shirt. If you was t' die t'night, you'd hafta be buried in that'n you're shakin' in right now."

Bertha heaved her two hundred and seventy pounds of multifolded suet from the chair and approached the bar. "Gimme a beer."

Mechanically, Ponce opened a can of beer and shoved it to her. She took it, and went back to her table where she sat alone. The others either drank quietly and listened to the approaching storm or talked in low tones among themselves.

CHAPTER NINE

When Uncle Henry got within sight of his house-boat-camp, on his return from his trip to the Chute, he was as drenched as he could ever remember having been. Several times he had had to stop paddling and bail water from the *pirogue*. His beer, now tepid, had escaped from its paper bag and scattered in the bottom of the boat. Rain came down in blinding sheets and thunder raved and roared overhead.

Uncle Henry shut his eyes against a lurid blaze of lightning that flickered and smashed a tree not a hundred feet away on the inside bank of the borrow pit. The detonation shook him and the light half blinded him.

Uncle Henry was not particularly concerned. Having spent most of his seventy years in the lap of the elements, it was to him just another storm to ride out, just discomfort that would disappear once he got into dry clothes. He was a trifle annoyed that his beer would be warm and he'd have to wait until it got cold in his icebox before he would enjoy it.

He stopped and bailed again, seeing as he did the dim form of his camp through a momentary rent in the veil of driving deluge. He massaged his gums together, stopped bailing and bent to his paddle. No need to bother with further bailing when he was this close.

As he nosed up to the raft on which the houseboat, long since unable to keep the water from its opened seams, rested. Danny opened the door and peered out. "Nice weather," he said with a grin. "Where you been?"

Uncle Henry said something under his breath and snapped, "Catch that rope and tie me up. Then you can throw me a bar of soap and I'll finish what the Lord started."

He undressed in the temperamental craft, a performance in itself, tied the stem carefully to insure better stability, took off his artificial leg and placed it carefully on the porch. He soaped furiously until he was a little ahead of the rinsing action of the rain, stopped and let the sluicing downpour wash the soap off, then clambered onto the porch.

"Now ... gimme a towel."

Danny handed him a towel and turned back to the stove which was giving off odors that Made Uncle Henry's nostrils twitch. Frying catfish.

He dried thoroughly, eased himself carefully through the door and onto the couch where he stretched out and relaxed. The day had been blistering hot but he was now cool and refreshed, no worse for his beer safari than a wetting which he had turned into a bath.

"Get that beer from the *pirogue* and put it on ice and however much fish you figgered on fryin', double it. I could eat you right now."

An hour later the beer was cold and the fish nearly eaten. Danny and Uncle Henry each opened a can and finished the sumptuous fish fry with long satisfying chasers of beer. Uncle Henry belched fastidiously and sighed. Life was good. His stomach was full, the day's sweat was washed from his body. He was cool and comfortable in his fresh clothes.

Danny dug into his barracks bag and brought out fresh khakis. "Think I'll do what you just done."

"Can't." replied his father. "Rain done stopped."

"The pit's fulla rain water. Where'd you put the soap?"

"Right out there on the porch where I clumb out. Did you run them lines at Patty-U Bend before you come in?"

"Sure did and at Charles Ridge, too. I put out one line right at that old rubber boat. That's where I cought that fifteen pound blue cat we just ate."

"We didn't eat all of 'im", protested Uncle Henry.

Danny chuckled deep in his huge chest. "We sure made a hole in 'im." He dived cleanly into the pit, swam around for a few minutes with powerful strokes, then climbed out on the raft and soaped down.

"This here fog is *some* thick," he called to his father.

Uncle Henry, too comfortable to reply, only grunted sleepily…then roused up. "What you reckon anybody's doin' out there tonight in a motor boat?"

"That ain't no boat," said Danny, striving to pierce the fog. "That's a airplane."

"Well,' said Uncle Henry complacently, "I'm glad it's him and not me. I wouldn't get in one of them things…"

"Good God," yelled Danny, *"He's comin' down."*

With a one-legged leap that belied his age, Uncle Henry lunged up and fell through the doorway.

"Comin *down?*"

"Sure…see them lights?"

The fog thinned and almost on top of them, it seemed. the plane skimmed along inches off the water, then dug in and flipped.

"Go get that man, Danny" roared Uncle Henry urgently, but Danny's soapy body had already split the water. He came up with a toss of his head and dug out for the fast sinking plane, the water boiling behind him. He reached the door and grasped the handle. Not knowing how it opened, he surged backward and ripped the door completely from the craft. As he did, the plane went under, its engine hissing as water steamed off hot parts.

Without hesitation. the big negro dived and went through the place where the door had been, feeling his way frantically. He found the man, located the safety belt buckle by blind intuition, snapped it loose and backed out, dragging the man with him. With a terrific surge and scissoring his legs powerfully, Danny worked his way to the surface with his man.

As he broke water, Uncle Henry yelled. "Here come a *bateau*. Catch onto it and heave him in."

The old man had untied a heavy fishing boat and with a powerful shove sent it scooting across the water. Danny grabbed the man in his thick hair and held him afloat with his nose just barely out of the water and waited for the *bateau* to reach him. He caught the gunwale with his left hand, struggled his feet to the surface, hooked a heel over the gunwale and rolled into the boat, still retaining grasp of the man. Then he caught him beneath the jaw and heaved him bodily into the boat. Uncle Henry tossed him a paddle which he caught and began to paddle for the camp.

"Is he drounded?" asked the old man anxiously.

"Don't know," said Danny as the boat scraped the porch. He tossed the man out roughly, followed him and turned him over on his stomach. He leaned forward and searched for respiration.

Uncle Henry, holding the gas lantern close, shook his head. "Not a breath. Better get t' pumpin' 'im."

"You go get Dr. Falcon," said Danny and began to rhythmically apply artificial respiration.

"He's at his camp?"

"He most generally is," snapped Danny. "Get goin'. I can't keep this up very long."

Dr. Anicette Falcon was a medical doctor who had tried to retire. His patients wouldn't let him, so he practically transferred his residence to his camp on the South Ramah borrow pits. Occasionally he would go out to Maringoin, a nearby town Where he lived to get fresh clothes and supplies, but he wouldn't stay gone very long. His camp was a few hundred yards further south than Uncle Henry's, so the latter didn't take long fetching him back.

He was a slightly built little man with dancing black eyes, intensely black hair. His unshaven face loomed dimly in the light. Uncle Henry steered the *pirogue* up to the porch and the old doctor leaped lightly out.

"Thought I heard a plane skating mighty low in the rain," he said. "Any signs of breathing, Danny?"

"Yes sir. He started not too long after Papa left, but it's pretty weak so I'm helpin' im' along."

"Good. I'll give him a respiratory stimulant." He opened his black bag and prepared a hypo with a speed born of fifty years of practice…found a vein with ease and pressed the plunger home.

"I think he'll make it all right now. Henry, break out some blankets. This boy'll be a sittin' duck for pneumonia before we know it…and he's got a nasty crack on the head. Damn, I wish we could get him to Baton Rouge and a hospital. This place ain't exactly what I'd want for pneumonia patient."

Uncle Henry looked dubious. "That levee ain't much of a highway wet as it is."

Dr. Falcon cursed in expressive French. "Man. that's a fact. That gumbo'd stick a Jeep right now. Well, we'll have to wait until morning and I'll run him up to Ramah in my boat and ring for an ambulance. Y'all'll sort of keep an eye on him, won't you?"

Uncle Henry looked insulted. "Now, you've knowed me long enough…"

Dr. Falcon grinned. "Okay, Henry, okay. I know you'll watch him. If he gets worse, come get me."

The same night that Charles Corbett Carraway, the Third, made his descent into the borrow pit on South Ramah, Marvin Denny returned from his stint in the Navy. He had changed to civilian clothes that fitted him well, he was tanned, mature and considerably filled out.

Shayne, not knowing for certain when he was coming, was just sitting down to a solitary meal when the taxi dropped him at her house. It *was* her house, Marian having taken care of that in her will. For no readily obvious reason, Shayne had never thought of the house as hers exclusively and she had never considered making them move.

On that night she indulged herself. She had grilled a small loin steak and being partial to French fried potatoes had prepared a lavish serving of them. A single candle supplied illumination for the meal and she had taken two bites when he rang the bell.

She made a grimace of distaste, got up and went to the front door.

He stood back well under the porch light and smiled at her. "Hi, Shayne."

"Marvin," she kept the eagerness from her voice by iron control. It wouldn't do to fling herself into his arms right at first ... if at all. "It's nice to see you. Won't you come in?"

"Thanks. From the smell I'd say you're eating or about to."

"Just two bites ..." Her face fell. "I'm sorry, but you didn't say when."

"I wasn't sure. Tell you what. If you'll lend me your car, I'll dash down to the store and get another steak. You finish yours in the meantime and you can watch me eat."

"That's a good idea," she said warmly. "Here are the keys. Bring back a fifth of good whiskey. This calls for a celebration. Do you need any money?"

He shook his head and laughed. "I'm loaded, kid. For a while at least. I developed into a mean poker player. I won over ten-thousand dollars in three years."

He was gone and Shayne had lost her appetite. When she mentioned celebration a raw flare of animal savagery seemed to blaze momentarily in his eyes. His face was good, though. Mature, handsome, and his body had filled out until he was a solid one-hundred-sixty pounds or thereabouts. Only his eyes seemed not to have changed.

Now that she could remember without emotion the occasion of her first and only kiss with Marvin, she could recall that his eyes had had that same hellish blaze on that night. She felt a little chilled. Maybe he was just that way. What way is that? she asked herself. Of a sudden a sense of shameless, gluttonous desire lashed her nerves into sickening heavy throbs. She recalled the judge's question. Would she?

She went into the dinette and put her steak back into the warmer. She still didn't know. What if he kissed her ... put his hands on her? She sank into a chair and shuddered. What was it about Marvin that did this to her?

Whatever it was that caused it ... Did she like it? Was is wise to allow it to get a grip on her? Had she been wise to suggest a celebration? Would she be able to maintain her equilibrium under such pressure as she had seen he could bring to bear? Did she want to maintain it? The thought made her muscles tense and the throb that lashed through her again made her weak and tremulous.

She had to know but what would the knowledge cost? She shrugged. Not more than she had to spare. Shayne did not view a fall with the attitude that some of her more strictly reared sisters shared. Every time she thought of the fall she could remember the time of that first kiss and the subsequent actions of Archibald. She had lost the effect of the shock ... the shock that she suffered when relative consciousness returned. She had not lost the effects of the shock of her first step into the padded red world of sensation. She would never forget the rending upheaval that blasted her into jelly ... into a state of physical nothingness that was like dying while yet learning what living was. A transient approach to the threshold of the pit, a shock that seared her nerve centers into temporary anesthesia.

This was what she wanted to know. What was it really like? What depths and heights were there that she had not yet visited?

She lit a cigarette and pondered over her thoughts.

If she had really wanted to know, couldn't she have had the experience times without number? She concluded that she could. It must be something else. A fascination provided only by Marvin? Was it an attraction she might regret and yet not be able to resist? Was it because she was just a little afraid of him?

Did the primitive streak in him attract her? Was it something stronger, something that might enslave her?

She stood up and threw her shoulders back, her eyes narrowing dangerously. *No* one would ever do that. With the upsurge of resistance she felt better. She sprawled out on the couch with defiance still shoving adrenalin into her veins, causing her to perform a pettish flounce. The act tossed her skirt high and it came down traitorously exposing one tan, satiny thigh in its entirety.

She raised herself on an elbow and regarded it critically. Without vanity she appreciated it. It was a surpassingly elegant limb and to be modest about it was a variety of dishonesty which was foreign to Shayne Bennett. She dropped a shapely long-fingered hand down, drew the leg up and let her fingers trace its healthy surface lightly. An unexpected rigor ripped through her, shaking her because of the unexpectedness. She sat up defiant and resenting the reaction. Again came, another kind of defiance to her. If she was highly sensitive, if as was true she knew she was beautiful, why, then, should she resent a thrill of self-appreciation? She laughed softly and relaxed. She was certainly full of questions tonight.

Relaxation seemed to stir her bodily responses more than tension. She forced a greater degree of it and closed her eyes nearly shut. Her breath came in a deep, regular rhythm, then a fever seemed to creep through her body. Her skin tightened to the sensation. Her breasts seemed to grow harder and quite without stimulation of an external sort the pink tips spiked high, so sensitive that the action of her respiration, raking them against the soft fabric of her light sweater, was physical ecstasy that amounted to pain in intensity. Her mouth flushed suddenly and she drew up into a coil on the couch. For some seconds she held to iron-like rigidity, then she relaxed and twin rivers of crystal tears scalded her lids and coursed downward.

She got up angrily and marched into the bathroom where she washed her face in cold water and with soap removed every trace of lipstick... her only cosmetic. She worked her lips in and out, burnishing them and reddening them by friction. Before she could ask herself any further questions, she heard the car come in the driveway and stop. A rocket of furious emotion rammed itself upward through her vitals, making her gasp and clench her teeth against it. She forced her face to calmness and waited for him, standing in the door of the kitchen.

He came in, negligently tossed the steak on the table and took her in his arms.

"I could feel it," he said huskily as he tasted the exciting heat of her lithe body from knees to throat. Shayne felt faint. Her breath came in labored gasps and her senses whirled like a vortex.

"Oh ... *Marvin.*"

His lips found hers and as they had done the first time her mind seemed to go blank to everything but the paralyzing ecstasy of the moment. Her teeth parted for the entry of his experienced kiss, her body welded itself into every line of his where she could force a retreat. Air whistled through her nostrils and her mouth twisted and raved upon his in a perfect agony of reaction. Guttural animal sounds forced their way from her throat to be muted by the ravenous devouring pressure of their lips.

Marvin withdrew for a moment somewhat stunned by her flaming response but not surprised.

Marvin still occupied his own little world, there being no room for anyone else and women just didn't do things like this to him. Her eyes were darker now, almost jade green, opaque and glazed. Her punished mouth was half open just as his lips had left it, tiny muscular reactions delivering the tiniest of twitches to hers.

"Good gosh," he thought. "Aphrodite herself, drugged and drunk with her own fever. No thought, no memory, no aim except to answer that soundless call that drowns every other sound."

Greedily he ripped at the thin sweater, the zipper that closed it close to her neck sprang open and the pressure of her breasts caused a four-inch gap to leap into being, revealing the warm, dusky edges of the magnificent mounds as they began their leap away from her chest. He moved his mouth into the humid canyon and then to the tip of one where he kissed it longingly with an intensity and a demand foreign to him. Her hands went behind his head and for a moment smothered him in the deep resilience that made his ears ring tinnily.

He stopped again and looked at her. She was now approaching the breaking point and the sadism with which he had been saturated all his life returned to shoulder aside the warmth and humanity that this marvelous creature had set in motion. Let her burn, let her be consumed in the conflagration which he had put into being. He put an arm around her and led her to the living room where he forced her gently to her knees on the carpet, then he knelt before her. With a sob she came to him and again their mouths feasted on each other until their heads rang and thundered with tumultuous blood that roared hot and red through their veins.

She went so weak that when he released her she sank back upon her heels. Her eyes were wet now and the sight almost routed the hell in his heart. Her lips were melting soft and wet, her eyes begging him silently. He slid his hands beneath the hem of her skirt and moved them slowly upward, caressing the wonderous skin of her thighs. She jerked as they touched her, her head went back, her back bent and one breast escaping from its covering sprouted upward, pointing almost at the ceiling. She rolled sideways and he fell forward, his weight crushing her to the thick carpet.

She knew in a little while that she had lost her sweater ... that she had lost her skirt ... that she had lost everything. Then she stopped losing ... thunderous heartbeats flogged unnoticed at her eardrums ... His skin seemed hot and fevered ... Then a livid sensation leaped through her ... hurtfully, then beneficently. It seemed to climb like the highest note on a violin, filling her entire being with a mad, screaming demand, a demand that her body answered with a response that chilled Marvin momentarily. She was like a leaping python, a naiad gone insane with nothing but release from this unendurable demand as her object. Her throat corded and veins stood out like purple vines. Her powerful body begging, entreating ... held for a paralytic four seconds, then collapsed in a death-like coma of relaxation.

Marvin recovered first and left the room. She lay on the carpet, a symphony of distorted sated grace, her soft hair spread in violent disarray. Her breath came in jerking sobs, then a hard rigor shook her with the authority of a malarial chill.

Marvin came back and did things of which she was only dimly aware, then he sat on the couch. He was winded, having been sorely handled. She had treated him as a powerful dog would a rag doll. She had struck him once upon a time a blow that nearly knocked him out. She had humiliated him beyond forgiveness. Now he had taken what he wanted from her and she was to give more. After a time she sat up, her eyes still heavy-lidded and stuporous, placidly inactive, unseeing. She shook her head making her heavy hair slide like a copper-gold waterfall over her bare shoulders, still unaware of her taped wrists and ankles.

Sleepily she looked at him and smiled. "I knew it," she whispered.

He nodded. He knew what she meant. "The first time?"

She nodded. "Marvin..." Her eyes found his and they were clear now and conscious ... reacting. "Marvin, I love you. I've wondered ... I've thought about it ... about you ..." She shook her head. "I'm no good at talking in a circle. I don't know any other way than to say what I feel."

"You'll feel plenty in a moment," he assured her, his voice hard and ugly.

She looked at him for a moment in a wondering way then noticed, at last, her taped wrists and ankles.

"Marvin, when did you do this?" She raised her wrists and examined them. "Why did you tape my ankles and wrists?" Her eyes sought his and saw the animal in them, the savagery, the merciless brutality that she had seen tiny glimpses of and hadn't recognized for what it was. It now flamed openly... without the careful protection he had accorded it in the past.

"Marvin..."

"You'll be saying that many a time in the next hour... or until I get through." He got up and pulled a heavy belt from his pants. "Remember how high and mighty you used to be?" The eyes gleamed in the dim light like a mad dog's. "Remember that time in the bathroom when you damn near killed me? Remember, when I'd try to make friends and how I finally bought... *me*, bought my way into your good graces. I've waited a long time for this." He lashed down with all his strength and the belt cut a wide red stripe across her back. She almost screamed as the scalding flood of pain poured through her senses. He was insane... Again came the belt and another stripe joined the first one and again she had to bite her lips to keep from crying out.

She was so shocked that the pain wasn't as great as it might have been. So soon after a journey into bliss that even the lashes could not embitter the rosy afterglow.

The distorted animalism of his face, the ugly insane gleam in his eyes, the bitter hatred that shone from them. How had he kept silent so long when the canker had been festering deep within him? She had been his, utterly, completely. Anything she had she would have given with all her heart. Again it came down and the tip slammed sickeningly into her side where her ribs offered no protection.

She became nauseated and thought for a moment she'd lose her dinner, but rage came to her rescue. Shame and humiliation fed it until Shayne Bennett was no longer a lovely girl, fresh and pliable from her lover's arms. She was a raging, fulminating cat, a wounded panther about to attack. She raised her wrists to her teeth and carefully seizing the tape in the correct spot, she surged backward just as the lash fell again. It cut her cruelly across the face, lacerating her upper lip and filling her mouth with blood. She would not cry out. He couldn't *make* her cry out.

Her strong teeth ripped the tape through and Marvin realized that he hadn't done a good job of it. In a split second she had ripped away the tape about her ankles and like a striking snake she came up off the floor.

She raged at him like a demon and Marvin reacted as he had not been able to make her. He yelled like he had been branded. Her first act had been to rake her right hand across his face slant-wise. Like the talons of a cat the nails ripped his face. This brought the bawl out of him and hardly had he voiced it when the left hand raked the other side of his face.

He was dripping with blood when she closed with him. She was a steel and whalebone tigress and though he fought with the peculiarly ineffective methods produced by panic, she gripped his throat like a constricting snake.

She was a pink and bronzed savage, fine long muscles standing out on her magnificent body, her teeth bared in a mask of hate and destruction, Marvin lost his balance and they crashed to the floor, the shock jarring her hands loose from his windpipe. She ripped at his neck, shredding the flesh and sending blood in rivulets, trying for another purchase but the blood had slickened her hands.

With an inhuman snarl, she seized his ear with her teeth and surged backward with all her strength, ripping it almost from his head before her teeth tore loose. He tried to scream but her hands had so punished his throat that it was little more than a raspy croak. She filled her hands with his hair and tore it out in hanks. A hand seized her own thick hair and she was jerked bodily backwards.

She rolled over and poised on finger tips and toes for a second, her eyes blazing with hate and desire to kill, facing her stepfather.

Archibald, unheard by them, had come in and unwarned by the devastation she had wrought, had pulled her away with a different purpose in mind.

In the second that she poised before him ready to spring, he knew that this was not the soft, delightful thing he thought, rather she was a wild animal on the loose with murder in her heart.

"Now...now..." He raised a protesting hand, his heart chilled to the core at the sight of those flaming green eyes, then she leaped.

In the split second that she had paused it had been turned off like a switch thrown. Gone was the heated ferocity that had seized her at first. Now came relative calmness, relative sanity but no mercy accompanied the throwing of the switch.

She stood and slammed the edge of her hand into the little hollow under Archibald's ear and jaw with every ounce of strength at her command.

A sickening crack sounded and Archibald folded up and went face first into the carpet.

Marvin was on his hands and knees retching and moaning.

She spun about and deliberately kicked him with all the power of her long muscular leg squarely in the throat.

He gurgled helplessly and rolled over, out and cold.

She stood over them for a moment, panting, disheveled, her cat eyes narrowed and burning. Her skin was flecked with blood and striped from the beating she had absorbed. She had the sure conviction that Archibald was dead. The thought caused her no remorse whatever. By doing so she knew that she had jeopardized her position in society. She felt certain that Judge Cross would come to her aid with whatever he could, but he wasn't the whole warp and woof of the sprawled and torturous body of the law.

She was not sorry for the act of killing him but something akin to panic claimed her.

She turned and dashed into her room, threw some jeans and shorts into a bag, dressed in khaki shorts, a blue shirt, a short denim jacket, and went back into the living room.

She didn't touch Archibald but assured herself that Marvin still lived, although he was considerably butchered man. Shamelessly she robbed his wallet of nearly five-hundred dollars and added it to her own fifty, then went to her car. It was full of gas, she knew, so that was a chore already done.

Without the faintest notion where she was going, she headed west across the Mississippi River Bridge, then realized that it was the most traveled and policed road she could have taken.

As soon as she could, she turned off through a field of waving sugar cane and drove south for a mile, coming to a smooth blacktopped road. She knew that to go east would bring her back to the river, so she turned west and drove along at a sedate pace. Then the reaction set in and she became violently ill.

She stopped, vomited, and started again. A chill struck her and she shuddered for thirty minutes before it ceased. She became nauseated again and had to stop. Stopping every five or ten minutes, making her way west by painful degrees, she finally found herself facing a high mound of earth ahead. There must be a road over it because she could see that it had been traveled.

Up the steep incline she went and had to brake hard when she saw that it was a levee and on top of it the road went north and south at right angles to the road leading to the crest. She felt sure now that she was at the edge of one of Louisiana's most formidable swamps. What better place to hide out? And they wouldn't be expecting her to stop so soon. She rode south along the levee but soon the gravel surface she had encountered at first ended and she was faced with a stretch of mud levee that she could see would test her driving to the uttermost.

CHAPTER TEN

Uncle Henry Pelichet, his patient gone to the hospital in Baton Rouge, sat and nodded in his camp doorway, his feet stretched before him. Danny paddled into the circle of light to the raft and got out of the *pirogue*.

"Well, how's the patient?" asked Uncle Henry.

"Middlin'," replied his son. "I guess they'll fix him up all right. The doctor says he didn't get much water. Just between me'n you I think that knot on his head was the most of his trouble."

"Reckon he'll try t' snake that airplane out?"

Danny shrugged. "Don't know. I don't think it was hurt much. Bent up some, maybe...who you reckon tryin' the levee tonight? They mus' think plenty of their drivin'. Right now I wouldn't want to drive a wagon on it."

"When you been livin' long's me," said Uncle Henry smugly, "you'll know there's ever' sorta person in the worl' you ever heard of. Plenty of 'em you aint' heard of."

"Well, I don't feel like doin' no pushin' tonight. I'm tired and hungry as a bitch wolf."

Uncle Henry dropped his pipe. "Now, whut'n you s'pose..."

The car as it neared the camp turned suddenly and plunged down the steep levee. Gathering speed as it came, it went into the bayou with a tremendous splash.

Danny leaped erect and began to tear his clothes off. "This here night swimmin's gettin t' 'be a habit..."

"Hold it... wasn't nobody at the wheel of that car." Uncle Henry muscled himself erect and holding to the doorfacing peered into the night. "See... up there... walkin' thisaway?"

Danny put his shirt back on with alacrity because he could see now that it was a woman. A woman walking limberlegged like she'd had too much to drink. She carried a suitcase.

"Sumpn's wrong with her," said Danny quietly.

"Sumpn sure is," agreed Uncle Henry but wrong or not he was not going to let his hospitality suffer.

"Go help her with that suitcase. Looks like she's cold and maybe hungry. Go on and help her."

Danny walked the narrow plank ashore and said as she came up, "Evenin', Miss."

She stopped and looked at him dully, shaking hard in the grip of another chill. She swayed and would have fallen but Danny sprang forward and caught her. Gently he lifted her and walked the plank with the ease of a trained acrobat, carrying her as though she weighed nothing.

"Put her on the couch... Great balls o' catfish," rasped Uncle Henry, his kindly heart swelling with rage. "Look what somebody done t' her."

"Somebody sure beat up on her, all right," agreed Danny, depositing her on the couch.

"Stuff that stove fulla all the ashwood it'll hold," ordered the old man. "I'll get a blanket wropped aroun' her."

Soon the stove began to give off waves of stifling heat, making Danny and Uncle Henry pop out with sweat. Uncle Henry watched her anxiously while the chill gradually subsided.

"Look," he said, "if we gonna roas', might as well make sumpn outa it. Put the coffee water on. Slide that *sauce piquant* up there where it'll get hot... and the rice, too. She might be hungry when she's feelin' a little better."

Later, still wrapped in the blanket with a few quivers of the chill still haunting the deeper reaches of her stomach, Shayne Bennett looked about her in dismayed surprise.

"Now, Miss," said Uncle Henry kindly. "Take this here coffee and whiskey. It'll take the jerks outa you quick like."

She took the offered brew and drank it gratefully but slowly. It was scalding hot and the whiskey seemed to penetrate every capillary of her body. Soon she was too hot and she threw off the blanket.

"Did my car go into the water?" she asked finally.

"It sure did," replied Uncle Henry. "How did you get out and how did it get away from you?"

"I did it on purpose."

"Well, now," breathed the old man thunderstruck. "What'n all the wide blue world did you do that for?"

She looked at the old man for a long time. He found her oblique green eyes direct and inquiring, but Uncle Henry did not have the kind of conscience that flinched from direct examination. He met and held her gaze.

"You've been very kind," she said in a throaty contralto.

"Yes'm. I'm a Christian man and I does what I can for my fellow man ... or woman, in your case."

"I want to thank you ..." She turned to Danny. "And you. too."

Uncle Henry with considerable acuteness decided that there was much more behind this occurrence than met the eye. Running a perfectly good, if not necessarily expensive car into the drink, a person of such obvious quality that it was instantly apparent, a savage beating, the reason for which was not apparent ... All these things raced through his fragile mind.

"I'm beginning to think I was a fool ... am a fool," she said slowly, looking from Danny to Uncle Henry.

"Some few's been that before you," said Danny quietly.

Uncle Henry nodded in agreement. "You couldn't get a patent on it, Miss."

All of a sudden Shayne realized that she was lonely, bereft of the understanding of a mother and alone in the world. These quiet, dignified colored men had befriended her out of the kindness of their hearts. They sympathized with her. Tears formed in her eyes as she looked at the older man.

"Somehow I don't think you'd tell on me."

He leaned forward, his face taking on a hawk-like cast, his soft brown eyes now as keen as drills. "I been known to be sensible and as for my mouth, it runs off when I tell it. Danny there'll do what I tell 'im."

She nodded. She suddenly felt safe and comfortable. She wanted to tell them … she needed to tell someone. So she did. She deleted the parts she knew would embarrass them and simply told them without mentioning names that Marvin had taped her wrists and ankles together and had beaten her with his belt. That she had torn loose and tried to kill Marvin, her step-father coming to the rescue. "And I killed *him*," she finished.

"With what?" asked Danny leaning forward.

"With my hand," she made a sharp sudden gesture with her hand, held blade-wise.

"Karate," breathed Danny amazed. "I read about it in a magazine."

She nodded. "But he's dead and they'll want me."

"Right from where I sit," remarked Uncle Henry, "looks like he was overdue for sumpn like that. You can count on us, Miss. We won't say a word but what'll you do?"

"I'm going into the swamp."

The old man shook his head and smiled. "You know the swamp?"

"No … I've never been in it."

"I been swampin' in for fifty years and I ain't seen all of it. You can't go in that swamp, Miss."

"I'll have to. They'll never catch me."

"Never is a long time," put in Danny with a frown. "How did vou figger on eatin' and such? You a good woodsman?"

She shook her head slowly. "I'm not much of a woods-man...put like that. I've fished and hunted a little. I can handle firearms very well."

"You got fishin' and huntin' equipment?" asked Uncle Henry.

"No."

"You got campin" equipment? Sleepin' bag, tent, cookin' utensils?"

"No."

"Then, Miss, how do you figure to live in the swamp?"

She shook her head distractedly. "You see, I told you I was a fool. I guess there's nothing to do but to go back."

"There's a side to that, all right. Maybe they'll figger like I do that the man was due to meet up with an accident. On the other hand..." He shrugged and Shayne knew that they weren't trying to get rid of her. They were intelligent men turning the possibilities over in their minds for her express benefit. They saw practical objections to what she proposed.

Uncle Henry turned to Danny. "Spray some o' that skeeter dope around. They's gettin' to bitin'."

Danny sprayed and Uncle Henry massaged his chin in thought. "You got any money, Miss?"

"Yes. Five-hundred an fifty dollars."

Danny chuckled. "Well, you sure didn't come with a naked pocket. I'll say that for you."

There came a soft grating noise at Uncle Henry's back and he turned to peer out of the doorway. In the circle of light sat Euphonia Unger in her *pirogue*. Uncle Henry didn't dare specu-late on how long she'd been there. Miss Phoney was something like a snake. You never heard her, you just saw her. Her big, lovely eyes were steady and her fabulous body outlined beneath her cheap dress was erect and steady as she sat in her boat.

"Evenin', Miss Phoney," greeted Uncle Henry shortly.

"Evenin', Henry," She spoke this time. Her voice was low, rich and evenly pitched.

"I been listenin'," she continued.

"We was afraid you was," he said slowly, wondering what to do ... what to say.

"If he's what she said then she shoulda killed him."

"Miss Phoney. I'm right proud to hear you say that. We don't think it'd be a good idea to talk it around."

"Fletch died, Henry."

"Well, now, I'm sad to hear it. When?"

"Las' night."

"Just took sick....?"

"Wine killed him. You know how he loved to drink."

"Yes'm."

"Now a minnit ago you was wonderin' what the girl could do, wasn't you?"

"Yes'm, we sure was. We hadn't thought of nuthin' fitten."

With the grace and surety of one long accustomed to cypress dugout canoes, or *pirogues,* Miss Phoney stood up, walked the length of the boat and stepped out as lightly as a feather onto the camp porch. Uncle Henry moved aside to let her enter and she stood for a moment looking down at the girl. Uncle Henry had never seen such a look in Miss Phoney's eyes and he marveled quietly as he watched.

"Honey," she began, 'I sure ain't got no palace out there in the swamp, but what I got you're welcome to half. One sure thing, there ain't likely nobody'll see you 'lessen they're lookin' for you. Eatin' is a pretty much of a sometime thing and it ain't town grub but what I got you're welcome to as long as you wanter stay."

Shayne stood up. Did she attract the best and the worst in people? Was she just lucky to have people help her when she needed it so desperately.

"I'm Shayne Bennett. I have money so we can buy what we need. As long as it lasts." Her brow clouded. 'My mother left me quite a nice bank account but I couldn't touch it now, I don't suppose."

Uncle Henry had a presentiment. This time he was elated because he knew what it was.

"Miss Shayne," he said, "you ain't got no way of knowin' what I'm about to tell you is true, but I think you'll be able to dip inter that bank account before long."

Danny nodded seriously. "When you hear him talk that way, you might as well set back and wait. He got a way about them things."

Shayne felt a stab of affection for the old man. "Thank you ... I don't believe your names have been mentioned."

"I'm Henry Pelichet and this is my son Danny. Most of my white folks calls me Uncle Henry. This here's Miss Phoney Unger. Miss Phoney, is you had the funeral yet?"

"Won't be none. I buried him in the swamp and said the Lord's Prayer over the grave. Fletch wasn't much of a churchgoer nohow."

"Do Mr. Ponce'n them know?"

"I told them tonight. Ponce said I done that right thing."

Uncle Henry nodded but he thought in his mind that it seemed a trifle callous to dump Mr. Fletch, even though he was nothing but a bag of wine-sodden skin and bones, into a hole in the swamp without benefit of clergy. It didn't seem fitting. But ... Mr. Fletch had taken himself a woman without benefit of clergy so maybe it was a habit with him. Maybe it was poetic justice or maybe God's will. Things didn't happen without it being God's will.

"Tell you what," he began. "Miss Shayne, you give me about twenty dollars and I'll buy up a nice collection of groceries from Mr. Joe's and I'll have 'em here for y'all tomorrow night and you can pick 'em up."

Shayne nodded in agreement. She impulsively took Miss Phoney's hand. It was surprisingly well kept and clean. "You're being very kind to me. I hope I can make it up to you in some way."

"You can do that by keepin' me company. It's lonesome as hell way back there at Tweed's Pass."

"Come high water," said Uncle Henry, "you oughta get somebody to pull you out to the front."

Miss Phoney shook her head. "Not long's this child is after by the law. We'll just hole up back there till hell freezes over. It's right neighborly of you, Henry, to offer to buy the groceries for us."

"That's what a neighbor is for and you know us cullud and white is been gettin' along for a long time."

Miss Phoney smiled a slow generous smile that revealed strong, white teeth. "Some as seems to say different, Henry."

"Yassum. Some as ain't got nuthin' better t' do. I'll have the rations here tomorrow night ... anything special?"

"We'll take your pick. Uncle Henry," said Shayne handing over the money and an extra five dollar bill. "Buy yourself some whiskey."

He took the twenty and handed the five back. "That puts a bumblebee up the shirttail of good intentions," he said solemnly. "Come Christmas or my birthday and you wanter drop me a little present, then I'll be right proud to accept it."

Shayne thanked them impartially and started for the boat.

"Better let me have that suitcase," advised Miss Phoney. "This here *pirogue* ain't the Queen Mary, you know. Now you set here on the bow seat and I'll swing the stern around and get in. Ever rid in a *pirogue* before?"

"No."

"Then be careful don't try to balance the boat. I'll take care of that. You just set."

With Shayne sitting carefully erect, Miss Phoney dug her paddle in with an expert twist and shot the boat at a sharp angle away from the camp. She crossed the borrow pit, pointed the nose up King's Ditch and disappeared into the black wall of the jungle.

"You know," said Danny ladling out a soup plate full of rice and *sauce piquant*, "this here place can be as quiet as a church on Monday then before you know it, *blam!* Ever'thing begins to happen."

"I knowed the other night I had the squirms about sum<a>n, and my stump had the prickles," said Uncle Henry nodding. "Plumb forgot to ask her if she was hungry."

"Miss Phoney slippin' up there quiet as a doe deer sure put the hot foot under me. You don't never know what people will do, do you?"

Uncle Henry snorted. "If you recollect, I was tellin' you sumthin 'bout that just before the lady's car went in the pit. First time Miss Phoney's spoke to me in a month'."

"I never figgered her as somebody who'd hold out a hand like she done."

"Comes a time," said Uncle Henry thoughtfully, "when your hand gets cold and you hold it out to warm it … by the sort of warmness that can't come but that one way. A man sittin' in jail in winter time all by hisself will get that kind of cold, too. Not bread alone it says in the Good Book and you could take that right on into other things. By *nuthin'* alone, you could say and you'd make many a one stop and think."

Danny nodded, feeling an old emotion that always accompanied the old man's philosophical wanderings.

"If you make people stop and think, you got a job done right there."

Uncle Henry knocked the dottle from his pipe. "Dish me up some rice and *sauce piquant* and put the coffee where it'll heat. Then I'm goin' t' bed … if don't no more airplanes light on us."

CHAPTER ELEVEN

Charles Corbett Carraway, the Third, opened his eyes in strange surroundings. The air had a peculiar sterilized smell; antiseptic and the walls were unrelieved white. Damn, he thought, a hospital. In a rush the events of his last few minutes of consciousness returned. He didn't move a muscle. Maybe he couldn't. Maybe he was broken into small bits and living on borrowed time. Maybe even now he was dying. Maybe this was the last crystal clear moment before final oblivion. Involuntarily he clutched the sheets. No pain. He moved an arm, then another. Still no pain. He lifted a cautious leg, then the other. He flexed his back gingerly. To all casual tests he seemed to be in order. A pretty nurse came into the room and arched thick black brows at him.

"So we're awake," she said with considerable accent, French, he thought. What would a French accent be doing in Louisiana? He phrased the question, more to see if he could talk than for information.

"My name," she said smiling, causing twin dimples to dip into sight in her cheeks, " is Angelique Falcon and my ancestors are Acadian. Maybe you never heard of *Cajuns, hein?*"

Charles blushed. I must be suffering from lack of memory, he thought. History was full of that miserable trek forced on French Acadians so many years ago. Evangeline, Longfellow and all that.

"I had forgotten," he said lamely and was then aware that although nurse she obviously was, with her stiffly starched uniform, and French she might be, she was undeniably pretty. "When did I get in here?"

"Last night. You're okay. Just a bump on the head and a little water swallowed. My Uncle Anicet brought you in."

"Who's he?"

"Oh … an old doctor who had to hide in the swamps so he could retire. He has a houseboat on Ramah."

"Sounds dismal. Where is it?"

"Right where you dumped your plane into the borrow pit. Don't you know better than to try to fly through a Louisiana storm?"

"I don't have sense to pour thumbtacks out of a boot." he said bitterly. "My actions prove it."

"Oh … it isn't that bad. By the way, your uncle is waiting for you to wake up. Ready to see him?"

"More than ready. I'd like to see the uncle I never knew I had."

A moment later Dr. Carmicheal came in, trim, dressed like a matinee idol in tropical blue pinstripe, Panama hat in hand.

"Ah … we awaken."

"We do," said Charles crossly. "Where did we come from so fast and since when were you my uncle?"

"You had me listed in your billfold as the one to notify in case of an accident. Dr. Falcon called me long distance last night from the hospital as soon as he got you registered. I took the company plane immediately. Got here nearly two hours ago. How is it?"

"How's what?"

"Your corporal self , your head, your lungs and ticker."

"Okay. I'd guess. What does the doctor say?"

"He said you'd probably wake up hungry and wanting to get the hell out of here."

"He's right on both counts. Can I go?"

"So he says. Said that prompt action by a couple of Negroes living nearby in a houseboat saved your bacon. One of them went under the water and dragged you out of the plane bodily. What were you doing flying through that storm?"

"I asked him the same thing," said the nurse, coming in with her chart and thermometer tray.

"I'm afraid that the only answer I could give wouldn't get me any applause."

"Well, if you think dunking yourself into that borrow pit got you any, I haven't heard it," said the nurse tartly, shaking down a thermometer. "Open up and suck on this device for a moment and we'll see if you're able to navigate. Open up now."

She turned to Dr. Carmicheal. "I hope you don't mind me shutting him up, but I'm off in thirty minutes and I have some other patients to see."

"Shut him up at any time," he said with a grin. "He never says anything. What do you suppose his excuse could be for flying so low?"

"Probably trying to read a racy novel and pilot at the same time," she offered.

"Nope. More like playing a game of chess with some ham with a shortwave set in Paducah."

"Or counting the revolutions of his prop and got hypnotized. All right, out she comes." She glanced at the thermometer. "I've seen cadavers in better shape, but the doctor says out you go to make room for someone who's sick. So get along with you." She turned to go but Charles called her back.

"I've known you about five minutes," he said carefully, "and I'm impressed."

"Most of my patients are impressed," she replied with a coquettish grin. "That's because I'm a good nurse."

"That's not what I mean," he countered, wishing desperately he was a really suave cCasanova who could lay the blarney on. "What I mean is … I'd like to see you again … soon."

The dimples deepened. "Say, you sound a little rusty. When was the last time you tried something like this?"

Charles flushed and swallowed. "Well, to be frank, I don't think I've ever tried it before."

"That's quietly obvious," commented Dr. Carmicheal heartlessly.

"All right, Charles, the Third. You may see me and soon. I don't think I could let such an example of a dying tribe escape my clutches."

"Let me warn you," put in Dr. Carmicheal to Charles' intense annoyance, "this man has shown his etchings. He is not to be trusted."

She stood sideways and drew herself up just a little. The delightful pout of her firm, young breasts took all the plainness from the uniform.

"I'll match him etch for etch," she said, coloring. "When will it be, Third?"

"Tonight?" he asked anxiously. "I'm wildly hungry and you could steer me to the biggest steak in town. The night would be yours and you could call the turns. Expense no object."

"You twisted my arm," she said and put her tray down. She pulled out a little note pad, wrote rapidly and tore out the sheet. "Seven-thirty at this address," she said swiftly. "Now I must be gone."

Charles looked stupidly at the name and address, then up at Dr. Carmicheal. "Uncle, did that just happen or did I dream it?"

"Well, nephew, I think you may safely assume that it happened, although I'm at a loss to know why. The girl must be on short rations and very hungry. Such glimmers of magnetism as you put forth wouldn't have shaken a Crackerjack compass."

Charles raked fingers through his tousled hair and sighed. "You know, ever since I resigned, I've been in a kind of fog. I left Houston, warned about the swamp and the weather. I forgot to file a flight plan, I forgot my check points and I lived three lifetimes coming through that storm."

"And since in that time you must have missed a lot you want to catch up in a hurry?"

Charles shrugged. "Something about that nurse took my fancy. So I was a little clumsy and fumbled like a ten-year old. I got the date, didn't I?"

"You did. Now that you got it you're going to lay there all night and mull over it, hunh?"

Charles started. "That's a good idea of how I've been thinking the last few days."

Charles got up and looked stupidly about for his clothes. He glanced at Dr. Carmicheal who was grinning.

"I'm not numb like you. I brought a robe of mine for the trip to the hotel. When we get there a haberdasher will have some clothes ready for you. You very thoughtfully had a tailor's guide in your billfold. Somewhat soaked but serviceable. By the way, weren't you the brave one … on a national tour with twenty dollars to your name? Or did you have some travelers checks stashed away somewhere?"

Charles pondered for a moment, a muscle in his lean jaw knotting spasmodically. " I had twenty-five-hundred dollars in a money belt … right behind me in the plane."

"Did ye now? Well, it's at the bottom of a very deep borrow pit or so the story goes. I guess I can let you have fifty cents or a dollar."

"You better cough up more than that. I told the girl that this was our night to howl … I don't suppose the doctor would mind, would he?"

"No. There wasn't enough water in you to douse a cigarette. That crack on the head didn't prove to be damaging. He says you're fit as a fiddle."

"Then how come did I sleep so long?"

"A drug know as Amytal … in the vein. Put you out so you wouldn't give any trouble and excite your head wound. After x-rays, et cetera, it was not found to be necessary but a good doctor doesn't trust to luck. Here, get this robe on and let's be movin'. You can take the gal by yourself since I have a dinner date with

Dan Woodward, the one I told you to look up. We're having wild duck gumbo with wild rice and wine, or maybe crawfish bisque with rice ... or something."

"Crayfish," corrected Charles, shrugging into the robe.

"Crayfish, my eye. I'm fro Gawgia, bud, and from there south a crayfish is a crawfish or if you like French, *crevisse*."

"You must have been around in your day, Doctor."

"You bet your athlete's foot I've been around. Now that I'm trying to launch you on a career of wassail and debauchery, I feel the old blood stirring. It wouldn't take very much to make me chuck that chairmanship and just quit cold like you did. I could sit on my can, play the market and still make more kale than I could spend."

Charles wheeled and caught the old man by the shoulders. "Look, Uncle ..." He choked and his eyes misted over. "What I want to say is, I'm not very much me, right now. It seems I'm still younger than I think. Simple things throw me. I know nothing about people in the common sense. I sure would love to have you come along. Dammit, I need you."

"Ummm," grunted the doctor, stroking his lean chin. "You sure need somebody. Well, I'll think it over."

That night was one Charles would long remember for a multitude of reasons. Angelique proved to exceed his previous assessment by so much that it was like meeting her all over again. Gone was her crisp, professional cheer and in its place was a warmth, a quiet pleasantness. Her hair was free from the white cap now and he could appreciate the stygian gloss, the soft thickness. It was shingle straight and she had made no attempt to use artifice such as curling or tricky barbering. She wore it in a soft feathery bob in the back, longer than usual, and the front was banged, but instead of a square it was heart-shaped, adding much to the piquancy of her mobile face. Her smile of welcome gradually faded but Charles didn't notice. He stood gawking at her like a smitten adolescent, his heart in his eyes, dumb with admiration.

"You still don't fit," she said softly. She approached, caught the lapels of his coat and gazed into his eyes.

"Er … what?"

"You don't fit. You don't know how to hide yourself. It's all right there in your eyes. You're telling yourself that you're in love with me and yet you couldn't be. We've had maybe ten minutes together. Third, I should be flattered but I'm not sure."

"Not … Why not? If you read flattery, then it was a good reading. You tie my tongue in knots."

The dimples deepened. "Thanks. The trouble is, people like you get hurt easily."

A thickening of his chest interfered with his breathing. "Yes … I've been hurt all right. Shocked, hurt … I'm still a kid, I guess, anyway you measure me."

"That's what I couldn't believe. Your uncle tells me you were president of Carraway Chemicals."

"That's right."

"How could you be president and …"

"I know what you're going to say. I had a top-notch staff, I had good advice and I never made a decision without getting a good cross section of opinion."

"But the final decision was yours."

"Well, yes, I guess so."

She turned away and picked up two highballs that she had previously made. "Then you're not the figurehead you try to make yourself. I think probably you're better than you have any idea." She smiled and Charles had to quell the desire to wriggle. "I must be frank. I never accepted any sort of proposition such as yours before in my life. You're *that* good. I kept asking myself all the way home, " Why did you do it, Angelique, why did you do it?'"

"Why did you?"

Her shrug called attention to the creamy elegance of her shoulders, revealed by a square cut off the shoulder blouse.

"Curiosity for one thing. I didn't think there were men like you anymore."

He tasted his drink, found it good and drank thirstily.

"That sounds like a good reason. I've read about women's curiosity."

She sat on a little hassock and looked up at him. "Haven't you ever considered that you might be sufficiently attractive to excite a woman?"

He shook his head. "No...I don't suppose so..." He found himself looking down at her, seeing the silent revolt of her breasts as they lunged against her blouse and the dark corridor that divided them.

"I hope," she said whisper-soft, "that you're still being complimentary."

He flushed red and sat on the couch. "One of these days," he said bitterly, "I'm going to have such control that loveliness won't throw me off balance and make me stare when I should have sneaked a quick look, then made a suave remark about the decoration of your apartment or something. It is pretty."

"Thank you. I doubt that I'd care much for the you you want to be, Third. You see, I like you as you are."

He grinned, relieved. "We've known each other only a few minutes."

"I know. I didn't say I loved you. Even if I did, I doubt that I could make myself say it on such short notice."

She finished her drink and bounced to her feet. "Here we are yakking away and I'll bet you're starved."

He nodded. "I could eat a whole steer, hoof, hide and horns."

"Then we'll go. Want a quick one before we do?"

"Please."

They each had a quick one and walked down the stairway, (hers was an upstairs apartment), to the car he had rented.

They ate heavily and well, Charles thrilling to see her eat with gusto, without pecking or pretense of diet or the need for one. In the soft light she was as angelic as her name. Again he found himself staring at the neck of her blouse which would gape a little as she leaned over to take a bite. He sighed and devoted his attention to his steak by force of will.

With the steaks had come a bottle of sparkling Burgundy and after dinner there was *creme de menthe*. What with the highballs he had had before eating, the wine and the liqueur, his head rang happily and the succulent filet dwelt richly amidst good company.

They rode for a while, Angelique showing him the city, the tall Capitol building, the University campus and stadium. It was all very interesting but Charles was in a nervous itch to get back to the apartment. His enthusiasm for the wonders of Baton Rouge must have been perfunctory and she had little trouble reading his mind.

"Why are you so anxious to get rid of me?" she asked after a little silence.

"Are you nuts?" he asked in surprise.

"Then maybe you're anxious to get back to the apartment or maybe you have an appointment."

"I have no appointment ..." He felt the heat rise to his face, glad that it was dark.

"Then it's the apartment. Third, what makes you think I'm the sort of a girl who'll ask a man up for a nightcap and possibly light dalliance when I've known you such a short while?"

He gripped the wheel and felt sorry for himself. How could a grown man be such a blunderer. "I don't guess I thought much about it," he said miserably. "I'll take you home now."

She was silent for a while. "Third, I think I was mean a while ago."

"You do?"

"Yes. If I get out of the car and bid you goodnight, you'll go on back to the hotel, won't you?"

"Yes," he was relieved. " Yes, I will."

"Then what was I saying that about you for? Maybe I'm naturally mean."

"No," he said, concentrating on being careful. "I think you probably read my mind…What I mean is, I did think of going back to your apartment, of having a drink and listening to you talk. You make such good sense. If I thought of anything else it was so far back in my subconscious that it never drew a picture for me."

She let go a soft liquid chuckle. "Third, I like you a lot…See that dark spot yonder under the live oak tree. Pull over for a moment."

He stopped, his mind refusing to consider why she had requested it. She came into his arms, fragrant soft, with that boneless urgency that women can affect at times which gives the impression that they're giving themselves wholly to the ecstasy of the moment. She did and her lips were petal-soft, mobile and so heartbreakingly sweet that Charles' chest ached fiercely.

Her mouth was a flower that opened for his and she swung her head gently back and forth delving deep, accepting his own searching efforts, clinging, her body finding his in all its detail. Then after some time had passed, she slowly withdrew. Her lips parted, her eyes glowing with a hidden light, her breath coming smoothly but faster than normal.

"Third, my boy, you've got it. Come now and let's have that nightcap."

She made them fresh highballs and again she sat on the hassock while Charles, not trusting himself to stand and look down, took the couch again.

"Why did you kiss me out there?" He made a vague gesture that embraced, roughly, all of outdoors.

She frowned at her drink. "I'm not sure. I wanted to, so I did. I'm glad I did. It showed me something about you."

"What's that?"

She made a little face at him. "I don't get you. In some phases of social activity, you're a bust. In others you're well, I wouldn't broadcast it, but back there under that oak you almost made little Angel make a fool of herself."

"Would that be a fool, Angel?" he asked softly.

She hugged herself suddenly, spilling a little of her drink.

"Don't ask me that, Third. I'm not good at smart repartee right now."

"What's wrong?"

"You ... and a lot of other complications that you don't figure in. I'm not being fair to you, either." She raised her head and he could see tears trembling on her long silky lashes. "This is all wrong. There I was going along just fine until I made a fool resolution to kiss you and it simply tore me apart." She shuddered and looked away. "I want to join you on the couch and I'm afraid to."

He slid from the couch and sat beside her. "I'll bridge the courage gap."

She looked into his eyes and saw the boy shining through but it was not a boy who sat at her feet now. She knew that like she knew the reality of firmament. With a low sound in her throat she fell off the hassock into his arms and their lips met, searching, eager, rabid.

Her hair became tousled and her body was unable to be still. She jerked herself away, stood up and clasped her face with her hands.

"There are so many things I want to say ..." She sighed and flung herself on the couch, giving way to a rigor that shook her thoroughly.

He slid over and placed a gentle hand on her head. "Go ahead and say it."

She turned her tear-streaked face to him and looked for a long moment. "I can't say anything. I'm twenty-four years old. I've even been called hard. All I know is that I'm not hard. When you kiss me, I'm putty. Third, I'm afraid."

He nodded a little sadly. "I understand, Angel. I'd better go now."

He stood up and she scrambled up after him. "Please don't go yet." She grasped him by the arms. "Please wait ... I don't know what for ... or maybe I do." She shook her head, making her hair dance. "I don't know anything anymore." She raised her head, her lips trembling. She strove hard to still them and failed. "Yes, I do know something, too, but don't have the guts to say it."

He grasped her shoulders. "Don't say it, Angel." He took her in his arms and kissed her again, almost wilting from the staggering bolt of sensation that sleeted over his body.

They parted to breathe and she clung to him, her face pressed against him, respiration making her breasts rake him, his nerves convulsing from stimulation.

"You were right. We don't have to talk about it."

"Not a Word."

"No talking, Third."

"No talking."

He picked her up and carried her through a doorway that had to be the bedroom. She didn't protest, only clung tighter to him.

He stood her on the floor and drew her into his embrace again and gradually began loosening her blouse from her skirt. Their lips still drawing agonies of sweetness each from the other, he let his hands wander over the smooth, flawless expanse of her back, finally finding and dealing with an obstruction. Her breath went out in gurgling gust ad she weakened in his arms, almost in a swoon. He caught her and let her slide gently through his arms to the bed, the act stripping up the blouse and with it the obstacle.

"Oh ... no ... " She gasped and covered her breasts with her arms. He sat beside her and took her into his arms again.

"No talking, Angel."

Automatically she moved her arms to embrace him and the touch of him against the supersensitive tips sent her into a shuddering rigor and a keening little sound came from her throat. She pressed against him so hard that he was afraid she'd hurt herself.

Suddenly Charles felt drained of energy, dry, beat out. He had been at an emotional peak for so long that his condition was not up to it. He reeled and sat on the bed, his face drenched with sweat and as pale as milk.

"Oh ..." Her hands went to her face, her eyes filling with tears. "I'm a hell of a nurse," she said in a hard voice. "There now, lay back and keep your head down." She had forgotten that she was nude from the waist up. Charles took several deep breaths and felt the blood coming back to his head. He put his arms about her and drew her to him. She collapsed and wept softly for a moment, then raised her head.

"Third, I'm through being a fool. What about a drink?"

"I think I need one," he answered.

She got up and stood looking at him and he at her. Her breasts were dusky pink in the dim light, spiking high and proud. She looked at them, then at him.

"Do you think they're lovely," she said slyly.

He croaked unintelligibly and nodded. She bent forward and offered first one then the other to his lips, collapsing in his arms when the sensation became unendurable.

She got up and fixed two drinks and they sat companionably and sipped the drinks until at last the same urgency made them both gulp and put the glasses away.

Vastly restored but determined to dally no longer, Charles sought electric connection with her mouth and while under its thrilling anesthesia, she was soon available to him, her skin soft, hot, her body telegraphing its eagerness. The shock of her body against his without obstacle made them both leap as though touched with flame. She tore her lips from his and gazed into his eyes, her own wide and at the same time frightened, questioning, passion-swept, then as nature with her unerring direction accomplished what she had sought, the anxiety and fear flamed out, leaving only a rabid demand. A long, ragged sigh seeped from her parted lips and she relaxed a little, savoring something, if not new, certainly a brighter newness than she had ever experienced.

Gone was the impression of feminine negativeness, of reluctance, of the willingness to let man be active and woman passive. He marveled at the strength, the momentary rigidity and the dead relaxed softness... the moments of raging action, like fire, that seared him at its point, then moments of exquisite sweetness when she was but a trembling supplicant torturing him with the agonized adoration in her eyes, the clinging ecstasy of her lips directed to him, telling him the age old story of woman's affinity for man, that he was her world, her firmament, the air she breathed, the drink that slaked her thirst... without him she was a shell, a nothing.

Without you, came an answering cry from his exalted soul, I am nothing, nothing is anything... All meaning must start with you, end with you, be contained in you, of you, for you, by you, because of you and in the absence of you... darkness, nothingness...

Dawn found them entangled, inextricably it seemed but on their faces was a peace that was transcendental. Simultaneously they awoke, looked into their eyes wonderingly, questioningly... then knowledge. Her arms tightened and she wept the clean, soft purge of utter poignant peace, in the backwash of heights that made her dizzy to recall.

Her mouth found his, entered and drank deeply and the quieted thunders began to mutter afresh in the distance, mounted louder and louder until a muffled cry broke from her lips and her embrace held a touch of hysteria, of a fearful joy that was so great that even the approach was terrifying. Only denial was more so.

Later, when the storm wore itself out afresh and shuddery peace descended upon them again, he became conscious of the little details of her that he had not had time to know before except as a whole. The deep, rich incense of her sleep-rested, passion-whipped body. The faint evanescent perfume from the disordered thickness of her hair, the throbbing bulk of her excited-hard breasts where they spread against him. The luxuriant curve of her slender waist that widened to accept the fecund generosity of her hips and the slanting reaches of her thighs.

Charles felt a sort of smashing awareness of everything that made up Angelique Falcon. He felt humble and unworthy before it. At the same time he felt a rare and peculiar hunger as though he would never get enough of her without some bizarre action…That of encompassing her entirely, like swimming in a pool of some liquid essence of her…so that he could be immersed in her sweetness, could massage himself and see her sink into his skin.

She could feel, could sense, the reaction that flickered through him like dull lightning…and in some manner knew how he felt. Possibly because she felt the same way herself.

Sometime later she stirred, and sat up.

"I'll have to go," she said tremulously. "It's five-thirty and I have to be at the hospital at eight."

"That's a long time," he said, never so proud of the smooth richness of his voice. Most of the time he had to speak carefully to keep his voice steady and melodious…to keep it from squeaking on the corners, embarrassing him. He sat up and slid his legs off the edge of the bed.

"But I'll have to bathe, dress, cook breakfast…" She bent swiftly and kissed him eagerly. She jerked away when things appeared about to get out of hand. "We'll never accomplish anything like this," she said gaily.

"That depends."

She went suddenly serious and fell to her knees. She rested her arms across his legs. "Third…I couldn't stand it if you thought this night was just another…" Tears came to her eyes, and she looked away. "Oh, don't think that I'm ... what I seemed last night."

He stood and lifted her to her feet. "Look here," he rasped, "you, last night, were everything any man has ever dreamed about. You wrapped the universe around us in this room. You were all things in all ways. I'll never be able to remember it without a sick tightness of the throat ... like just before shedding tears. Last night may be the closest I'll ever come to immortality."

She looked up at him. Her eyes wet and enormous, like deep stygian wells. "Third ... I didn't believe you could do it. That's the most beautiful speech I ever heard. You mean it, too. I couldn't be wrong about that."

"You shouldn't be," he chided. "You were wrong in your first remark."

She fixed breakfast for them. Smoked sausages grilled slowly, fluffy scrambled eggs, hot biscuits and a kind of coffee with which Charles had had no experience. The first gulp almost crossed his eyes. Two cups, he felt, would get him on another binge.

When they finished, Charles was conscious of another new reaction. He was becoming food conscious. This breakfast had dealt him several new taste sensations. The hot buttered delight of freshly baked biscuits, the tingling of country smoked sausages that had more than a speaking familiarity with red pepper, and *that* coffee.

He stopped eating for a moment, watching her as she ate, concentrating on her food, or giving the appearance, her pajama coat open at the neck revealing dimly shadowed vistas that were more appealing when cloaked with mystery. What he couldn't see, below the table top, was even more intriguing. She wore only the long pajama coat—nothing else.

After breakfast she puttered around putting away the dishes and clearing the table. He sat and watched her until he could stand it no longer.

"Angel?"

She spun about making the jacket flare dangerously, her hair switching to the quick movement.

"Come here."

He moved the chair away from the table and she came ... covering him like a cloud of warm, stinging incense ... smothering him with a flood tide of wonder ... the same that had rent him so sorely during the night and the early morning and yet new ... new like a fresh rose that becomes fresher as the dew falls, that brightens and lifts an eager head after the shower.

CHAPTER TWELVE

D r. John Weatherspoon Carmicheal, sitting up in his hotel room bed, was eating a pasha's breakfast, slowly, deliberately, with much smacking of lips and unnecessary loss of motion. A tremendous tray was in front of him with legs reaching to the floor to make it unlikely that the arrangement would topple and drench the feaster. He was clad in tissue thin black pajamas, the jacket open down the front. A tiny particle of butter rested untidily amidst the grey hair of his chest, a silent reminder of his slothful carelessness.

He lifted a hot lid, took out another light tender roll and buttered it with care, clamped it shut and returned it to its warm nest. His three scrambled eggs had disappeared some time ago but this was his second serving of rolls and before him lay another serving of five more slices of crisp bacon. A pot of coffee snored quietly on the hot plate at his elbow on a small table. He was pouring another cup of the several he had had when his newest nephew stepped into the room.

Charles looked and his eyes widened. "What is this, a ceremony honoring the god of breakfast?"

"Nup," said the doctor, blowing on his hot coffee. "Just an old southern custom. When a man orders a breakfast like this nobody faints or falls down the elevator shaft. Dammit, I've been up in the badlands so long I forgot to order grits. I knew something was missing."

"As a cereal, grits hasn't much to recommend it," said Charles helping himself to coffee.

"As a cereal, you are perfectly and offensively correct. It was never intended to be a cereal in the first place. It's a breakfast dish with guts when running yellow with butter or red with ham gravy. A fitting companion for eggs, bacon, ham, sausage, smoked pork loin, *boudin, andouille*... Hell, there's no use telling you all this. You haven't the foggiest notion of what I'm talking about."

"You're a different person," said Charles with no small amount of wonderment in his voice. "You even talk differently."

"Son, I'm really relaxed for the first time in years and just now have sense enough to know it."

"Then you're going to stay...?"

"And wet nurse you? Yap, I am. I know too much and you don't know enough. I'm writing them a long telegram when I get around it. No rush. By the way, we're taking over Dan Woodward's camp out on Ramah for a while. He'll check it today and see if the provisions are up to snuff and the deep freeze sufficiently stocked."

"That doesn't sound much like a camp... with a deep freeze."

"A man doesn't have to suffer to camp. Actually, he says it's a hell of a nice cottage resting on a steel barge and tethered with steel ropes to a couple of willows. They run an electric line from the nearest power cable which ain't far and he has all the comforts of home. Think of it, Nephew, you get up, make coffee, drink it, have a lazy cigarette, then dive off the bow and take a quick cold swim. While that's goin' on, you get a bitch of an appetite, then you come in and load up."

"Who does the cooking of all this fine food?"

"Your uncle. That's something else about me you didn't know. Not only that, even Uncle is in for some culinary surprises. Last night we had none of the wonder of which I spoke, although they are wonders as well. I had flounder, stuffed with shrimp and crab meat, seasoned with herbs, garlic, saffron, basted down in a lemon butter sauce and barbecued slowly over hickory coals.

Mother of manna, what a feast. By the bye, we might as well go down and find us some sort of all-weather car like a Jeep or something. Dan tells me the levee gets pretty rough sometimes in wet weather."

"All right. I'll write a draft..."

"Dan will speak for us. They'll take our paper without question... Saaay, what the hell happened to you?"

"Er... Me? Nothing. Why?"

"Well, for one thing your bed ain't been slept in. For another you talk like a man with some portion of a brain this morning. You're letting me order your life without a protest."

Charles turned scarlet. "Let us say that paradise was visited and let it go at that."

"Ahhh. That way, eh? Well, for a stumbling, only partly coherent cCasanova, you did right well, it seems... and I know whereof I speak. Our Angelique is no tart. That gal's quality; high on the hog."

Charles' throat tightened. "You don't know how glad I am to hear you say that. I had a puritan termite eating at me and didn't realize it until you spoke. You cleared things up a lot."

"Oh, my aching sacred lilac," snarled the doctor. "If I ever see such a termite in action I'll take considerable delight in stomping the guts out of it. Grow up, boy, grow up. I'll admit that you covered a lot of ground in a short while and you weren't used to it. Let it go at that."

Charles put down the coffee cup and said in a low voice. "She sort of made a prayer at large that I not think she was what she seemed last night."

"And if you had the guts of a fly and the sense of justice of a catalpa worm, you busted an intestine to try to show her *exactly* what last night was. If you left her aching over what overwhelmed her, then you can get up and go make amends..."

"You'd have been proud of my speech. I can't even remember it, but her eyes were glowing and wet when I finished."

"Now ... that's my boy," said the old man, his voice soft with affection. "There are a few of us, son, who tickle sin because sin tickles us. We have to have the guts to carry it off and we have to have the principle and the ethics to see to it that we don't leave any ash piles along the road."

"I got a taste of that with Edna, the maid," said Charles, the memory bringing back the old ache. "I offered to marry her. She wouldn't have me."

"And one reason why she wouldn't is because she knew that deep down you offered it to make an 'honest woman' out of her and she had no sense of dishonesty. Make you a bet on that."

"You may be right." Charles sat up straight. "Look, will I be bowled over by every pretty face and figure that ..."

"Hold it ... hold it right there. There've been two. I know both of them. Name me another two that could touch them in looks, plain common savvy and levelheadedness. Go ahead. Name ... Hell, name me just one."

Charles shook his head. "I don't guess I can."

"No, I don't guess you can either. Now let me tell you something. The day that you can't react to quality like that, loveliness that it its own excuse for existence, superiority, human excellence ... when that happens to you, Bud, you might as well walk off in the river and take a deep breath. No, I don't think every one of them will bowl you over because one of these days you'll find one that'll clip you so hard she'll be your whole sky from horizon to horizon. You'll be able to notice the others and appreciate them, but their old power will be gone."

"What can happen to me in Ramah swamp?"

"Well, we ain't sentenced for life and there's many a fine gal all around Ramah swamp ... and from what Dan tells me there just might be some in it. He was telling me about a fine amazon of a woman who sort of took up with a swamp rat. He was sorta secretive about it. She must be sumpn the way he described her. She is, accordin' to him, rape in a *pirogue* or sumpn like that."

"Get out of bed and let's see about the Jeep. I got to return the rent car, too."

Danny sat on the porch of the camp and yawned. "No kind of fish bitin' today," he complained.

Uncle Henry came to the door and looked critically at the weather. "'Nother one of them trash floatin' rains comin' most likely. You run them lines at Patty-U Bend?"

"Yassuh."

"Them back of Charles Ridge?"

"Yassuh. You seen what I brought in. Fifteen little channel cats...ten gous. For all the paddlin' I done, I oughta had a boat full."

"Sometimes it's like that. Looks like a shame that expensive airplane lyin' on the bottom of the pit there. Bet we could pick her right up with the sinker boat."

Danny grunted. "That light thing? Snatch her up from there like nuthin'. If it'll pull up a raft of waterlogged cypress logs, it'll sure pick up that light thing. You know, that's a good idea. He might just love to have it pulled out and you know what it'd cost him to bring people all the way from Baton Rouge."

Danny stripped to his shorts while Uncle Henry carefully maneuvered the unwieldy sinker boat into position. Danny, after measuring for location against the opposite bank, a certain willow tree and the houseboat, coiled the rope around his left arm, tiptoed and went into the water like an otter. For some time he stayed under, then surfaced and blew like a whale.

"What'd you hitch onto?" asked Uncle Henry as he reached for the rope.

"That little thing what supports the tail wheel. When I got down to it I had to study for a while and that was the only thing I could think of to hitch onto. Them wing braces wouldn't have done right and might of tore the wing up. The propeller end might of disjointed the motor or sumpin. By bringin' her up tail first and easy, oughtn't to hurt anything."

Uncle Henry made the rope fast to the windlass after passing it through the boom pulley.

Danny clambered aboard. "Don't take up the slack yet. Le's get the boat to land, anchor her good, then work the windlass. Soon as we get her up close to the bank, I'll get Mr. Eddy to run up here with his Jeep and we'll snake her out on dry land."

In less than an hour's time the sleek, if somewhat battered Cessna was dripping water like a sieve but sitting comfortably upright and on dry land.

"Not much trouble," said Uncle Henry with satisfaction as he watched Mr. Eddy's jeep climb the levee and disappear toward Ramah.

Danny dived again, recovered the door he had ripped from the plane and tried to replace it temporarily but he had done too good a job.

"Boy," breathed Uncle Henry as he looked at the ripped hinges. "You musta sorta come back on that thing."

"Had to," said Danny dropping the door and peering curiously inside the plane. "Didn't have no time to try t' figger that latch out. See it's sorta sunk into the…" He took an involuntary step backward then chuckled. "Now that's a funny lookin' thing hung over the back of the pilot's seat. For a minute I thought it was a snake." He reached inside and took out a water-soaked money belt and hefted it. "What you reckon this is?"

Uncle Henry took it from him and inspected it, finding that it closed with a zipper. It stuck momentarily, making him exert more than normal effort, then suddenly it gave and a cascade of soaked bills fell to the grass.

"Great palls o' red oak twine," ejaculated Danny, his eyes widening.

"I'll be a suck-egg crawfish," contributed Uncle Henry.

They got down on the ground and after much careful effort soon had it spread out in the sun drying. Twenty-five-hundred dollars lay in the hot sun and began to crinkle and curl. Uncle

Henry sat on a log nearby and eyed it with satisfaction. "Well, it don't hurt none to sit here and examine a busted bank. I ain't never seen so much money in one spot in my life."

Danny, stretched on the grass beside his father, said, "Bout dry. Ain't it pretty? Guess that man's luckier than anybody I know."

"How's that?"

"Well, he cracks up in the borrow pit and there I is all ready and waitin' t' pull him out. Then we pulls the plane out and unless I'm no judge, it ain't hurt too bad. He loses a money belt along with his plane and we find it and dry it out for him. What if a coupla hundred men you can call to mind right now had found that money? Think he'd ever see any of it again?"

Uncle Henry nodded so vigorously that his pipe fell from his gums and he caught it deftly with his right hand. "That's a fact ... looks like somebody comin'."

It was a Jeep station wagon, brand new but the driver curved it off the crown of the levee and let it roll down to the camp dock. It stopped and Charles got out, followed by Dr. Carmicheal. Charles walked over where Uncle Henry and Danny sat. He stopped and looked at them for a moment, not recognizing them but feeling certain they must be the ones he sought. Both men got to their feet and Uncle Henry never long without command of his tongue said, "Well, it's sure fine to see you lookin' so good. You sure didn't look good when you left here the other mornin'."

Charles said, "Then it was you two ..."

"Yes sir. My son Danny here fished you out. We sent for Dr. Falcon and him and Danny got you out and inter the hospital. Wasn't a lot I could do cause I got a wooden leg."

Solemnly Charles shook their hands. "A man always sounds like a fool when he tries to thank someone for saving his life ..."

"Things sometimes get a little big for a man's tongue," soothed Uncle Henry. "It ain't necessary for no thanks."

"Just the same you have them and if there's ever a chance, I'll try to pay you back. Money I've got a lot of, but money falls short of what I mean."

"Oh, money ain't so bad," said Dr. Carmicheal coming forward and shaking hands with Uncle Henry then Danny. "Allow me to add my thanks. This boy's no kin to me but I've sort of adopted him. I see you've snaked the plane out."

"Along with a bank robbery," said Danny with a grin as he indicated the drying money.

"Good Lord," said Dr. Carmicheal. "You found the money belt?"

"Danny thought it was a snake at first," chuckled Uncle Henry. His expression changed. "Shame on me... Didn't tell you gentlemen our names. I'm Henry Pelichet and this is my son Danny. White folks mostly call me Uncle Henry."

Dr. Carmicheal frowned thunderously. "Not me. I'm too old. Older'n you likely."

"How old?" asked Uncle Henry slyly.

"Fifty," boasted Dr. Carmicheal, "and don't feel a day over thirty."

Uncle Henry grinned. "Well, I ain't but seventy, but I'll thirty with you any day."

Charles laughed. "Well, you're both too old for Danny and me, hunh Danny?"

Danny was undecided.

"It don't pay t' underrate that old man there. Sometimes he'll surprise you. For instance, two hours before you went in the water there, he knew sumpn was fixin' to happen."

"Mind you," continued Danny, starting to retrieve the money, "I ain't superstitious myself... I'm just tellin' you what happened. It ain't the first time either."

The money being curled and distorted, refused to go back into the belt, so Danny found a twelve pound Kraft bag and stuffed it. "Well, like I was tellin' Papa just before you got here, you's one lucky man." He handed Charles the money.

"I'm lucky, all right," mused Charles hefting the bag. "More ways than one." He handed the money to Uncle Henry. "Take it. There's plenty where it came from."

Uncle Henry shook his head adamantly and handed it back. "No sir. I don't take pay for bein' a human bein. Danny don't neither. The Lord made us humans and if one human can't hold out his hand once and a while, then the world done come to a bad way. No sir, and no disrespect intended, let me make you sure. Now just between friends, if you got sumpn you think I might like and you're feelin' free, like a fine fifth of licker or some little lie-low-to-ketch-meddlers like that, then I'll be happy to accep' it ... Thank you, sir."

"Well, I'll be a triple plated rhinoceros," said Dr. Carmicheal to whom a casual attitude toward money was to be viewed as a major affliction. "Dammit, Henry, take the cussed stuff. The boy's got more'n he'll ever see."

"No sir," said Uncle Henry with concrete stubbornness. "Thank you, sir, I'm sure, but what I do for my God and what I do for pay is two different things. If I do a day's work for you ... lessen it's just a favor, then I'll expec' to get paid. What me'n Danny done wasn't no more'n the Lord would expect one of his children to do for another'n. Thank you, sir, but we don't take money for things like that."

Charles looked at Danny. "Er ... Danny ... "

"Papa speaks for the family in most things," he said firmly. "Like he said, if you got a oversupply of sumpn some times and want to drop us a little present, that's fine but not for pullin' you outa the water."

"But what about pulling the plane out?"

"That took a hour of time we had to spare," said Danny, entering the spirit of charity. "It wasn't no trouble and the fish ain't bitin' nohow."

Charles and Dr. Carmicheal looked helplessly at each other. Finally the doctor turned to Uncle Henry.

"Henry, we've been living around the wrong people too long. We didn't think there was any more of your kind left."

"Get off that boss, Doctor. 'Less I miss my guess, you's my sorta people yourself."

Dr. Carmicheal colored. "Well, don't advertise it. I told this boy this morning we'd lived in the badlands too long. By the way, do you knew where Dan Woodward's camp is?"

"Mr. Dan's ... Sure I does. Right yonder ... just this way from Dr. Falcon's." He pointed a finger.

"Best camp on Ramah. Tell you sumpn ... er ... you knows Mr. Dan well?"

"Like a brother. Me'n him went to school together."

"Well, then you knows that there just about ain't a better cook in this country'n Mr. Dan. Not even me and I been knowed about as a cook."

"I know that. I had dinner with him last night ... Excuse me, Henry, I mean supper."

Uncle Henry laughed heartily. "Them badlands is dyin' out in you, all right. You sound like a man what's come home."

"That's exactly how I feel, believe me."

"I believes you. I ain't very often wrong about men."

"He ain't *never* wrong about men," amended Danny, who seemed to be thinking of a time when he had been wrong and Uncle Henry had been right. "Y'all goin' to Mr. Dan's camp?"

"He's let us have it for an indefinite period," said Charles.

"All right ... You got any stuff?"

"Plenty," said Dr. Carmicheal.

"Well, we'll put it in this here *bateau* and I'll paddle you over."

Dr. Carmicheal had spoken the truth and their dunnage nearly filled the boat. Last among the load was a heavy cardboard box which the doctor attacked as soon as it had been stowed aboard.

"You mentioned a fine fifth," he said to Uncle Henry who stood by supervising. "Try your lips around this. Bradsher's Special Age."

"Looka *here*," said Uncle Henry manifestly more pleased with the fine fifth than he had been with the green cash. "Thank you, sir, and if it don't cast a spell I think I'll sample it right now."

He unstoppered it and took a long pull. "Ahhhh", he breathed. "Sure would be a sin to use a chaser on this fine stuff. Thank you again."

The doctor put down a second fifth for Danny and they got carefully aboard the bateau.

The cabin rather amazed Charles with its luxury. It was not, of course, home luxury but certainly no one would have cause to complain of this abode. It was on a huge steel barge, one tremendous room that was living, bedroom, dining area and kitchen all in one. In the back was room for a shower and a large cistern that caught water for drinking and cooking purposes. Also in the back was a butane tank for heat and the kitchen stove. Inside there was a large gas range, sink, refrigerator and a twenty-foot deep freeze. Dr. Carmicheal opened it and found it stuffed with food. Some already cooked and cartoned. Some ready for cooking.

The entire room was carpeted with a thick rugged hemp mat that was impervious to water and stain. It was old and had aged into a dull dun color. There were three comfortable beds, two big plastic-covered couches draped with colorful Navajo rugs and numerous chairs of no particular pattern. Dr. Carmicheal dropped into one huge cane-bottomed rocker and leaned back.

"Boy, it's been many a day since I unlaxed in one of these. I reckon my mother must have rocked me a million miles in my time."

"This place is sort of overwhelming," said Charles looking around. "Are we to just take over?"

"Sure. Dan'll be down occasionally but he can't take up but one bed and we'll feed good while he's here."

Danny helped them store their possessions and they gathered on the front porch. The sun stood at the zenith and blistered the dancing waves of the borrow pit.

"Scorchin' out there," said Danny, wiping the sweat from his forehead with the back of his hand. He turned to Charles. "You much of a boatman?"

"Not much."

"Hunter?"

"No."

"Fisherman?"

'No. I don't guess I'm much good at any of those sports. I never followed them."

"Well, the difference in them as does and them as don't is whether you want to or not. Think you'd like it?"

Charles nodded eagerly. "I sure would."

"Then you got yourself a teacher." Danny grinned engagingly. "Just 'tween me'n you, you got a good teacher."

"Looks like you're good at a lot of things, Danny," said Charles.

"Lemme brag on my own self," said Danny in confusion. "What you got to learn first is how to ride in a *pirogue*. In a *pirogue* I can take you plumb to the 'Chafalaya River as long as I got a little mud or a heavy dew. You get set and I'll take you to run my lines and show you the tricks. We better use bathin' suits the first time cause we're likely to get wet." Danny pawed in his thick, curly hair. "Y'all hear anything about a killin' in Baton Rouge last few days?"

Charles shook his head and Dr. Carmicheal snorted. "We've been out of touch the last few days and all I read a paper for is the comics and baseball. People are always killing one another. There probably was a couple of murders. Why are you interested?"

Danny waved a hand vaguely. "Oh … nuthin'. Just heard some talk … just a rumor most likely."

Danny went back to the houseboat and sat for a moment smoking and gazing abstractedly across the sky.

"Got sumpn on your mind?" asked Uncle Henry, blowing on a cup of hot coffee.

Danny sighed and blew out a cloud of smoke. "Can't get that little girl off my mind. Looks like if she had killed that man, it'd be in the papers.

"I looked in one this mornin'," replied Uncle Henry, "didn't see a thing."

Danny shook his head. "You know, could be that man ain't dead at all … and Miss Shayne is runnin' for nuthin'."

Uncle Henry put down his coffee cup. "What was that judge's name she mentioned?"

"Cross. I knows him pretty good. I've taken him duck huntin' a couple of times."

"S'pose you go to Mr. Joe's and call him up. The way she spoke of him he was on her side."

"Think I'll do just that. That'd be one good way to get it straight. I'll just talk around in a circle to see if he knows anything. I won't tell him nuthin' unless I see it's safe."

CHAPTER THIRTEEN

Shayne Bennett sat in the shade of the little drop roof that covered the tiny porch of Miss Phoney's houseboat. It, like Uncle Henry's was old and now depended on a huge raft of cypress and gum logs for flotation. Miss Phoney had thrown a quilt over one big log and was sprawled face down, naked and relaxed, letting the fierce sun beat on the broad expanse of her magnificent body. Shayne felt a ripple of affection go over her. In the few days she had been Miss Phoney's guest, she had discovered something innately fine about the woman. Something she had not expected.

Shayne got up and stripped to her skin. "May I join you?"

Miss Phoney stretched like a jungle cat, raised her head and grinned. "Sure, honey. Get another quilt to keep the knots outa your hide. Take that big gumlog there. You like the sun, too?"

"Not as much as you do, I don't think. Doesn't it dry your skin out?"

"Not so's you could notice it. If I told you how much I love the sun on my nekkid skin, you'd think I was some sorta queer." She sat up and crossed her legs, leaned back, letting the rays caress her neck, breasts and stomach.

Shayne stood over her and looked. "You know something, Phoney? You're some fine hunk of woman.'"

Miss Phoney colored a little. "Yeah, and it's goin' to waste out there. I wish a good, stout man would happen along. I could use one."

"Just any man?"

Miss Phoney shrugged. "Lessen he was dirty... or a fool... or mean. I don't think too much of me when I look at you."

Shayne smiled and lay on her back, letting the sun beat down on her. Miss Phoney got up, walked to the edge of the raft, plucked two water hyacinth leaves and deposited them over the tips of Shayne's breasts.

"Don't never get sunburned there, honey," she advised. "They can be mighty painful."

"Thanks," said Shayne, luxuriating in the harsh bite of the sun. Her skin tingled and the warmth crept in deeply. She thought back over the last few days of her life and her muscles grew taut with anger... then the thought of the wonder of her first experience of the deeper shades of love. A shudder quivered the muscles of her stomach and her breath came faster.

Detail by detail she relived it, the electric wonder of her kiss... she frowned, revolted. She had seen Marvin at long last as he was and even the thought of him sharing her ecstasy made rage boil within her. She obliterated him from her thoughts and substituted a fair-haired giant, handsome and gentle, with an amused mouth and crinkles at the corners of his blue eyes. Miss Phoney sat up silently and watched Shayne take herself through the entire spectacle. Watched the fine globules of sweat that broke out on her skin, watched the subtle motion that activated her musculature... watched love mount in her mind until she shared it with her physical self and finally drew up in a ball and hugged her knees hard.

She sat up quickly, a scarlet flush dyeing her whole body. Miss Phoney nodded slowly. "I wondered about you. I think I know more now."

"It... sort of took me away... for a moment," murmured Shayne apologetically. "I forgot you were here."

"It wasn't all pleasant, was it?"

"No ..." She looked at the older woman. "I'll tell you ... all of it." And she did.

Miss Phoney didn't speak for a long time, then said, "Shayne, in a lot of ways you're like me. I guess I'm a pretty peculiar person. I don't live by the rules much, but I live like I want to. Would you believe that I come from a good family in Alabama, that I attended the University ... and yet look where I am."

"I knew something like that was true ... I felt it, maybe I should say. You've been speaking better and better since I've been here."

"Yes, I suppose so. It's easy to fall into bad habits."

"How did you ever get out here?"

Miss Phoney sighed. "Like I said, I don't live by the rules and that didn't fit with the ideas some other people had. I was expelled and I didn't want to go home. I was ashamed, I guess. Then I got drunk. Who knows what I did or where I went, but when I finally came to my senses I was in a little backwood's bar not far from here drinking wine with the man I buried a few days ago. He wasn't such a winehead then, he had teeth and was kind in his own way. I was heartsick and had no place to go. He brought me out here and until a few months ago, he made me as good a husband as he was able. I was pretty cruel to him, I think I subconsciously blamed him for some things that were my own fault. I became a swamp rat in mind as well as in body. I've rolled in the hay with some of the young bucks when Fletch got too weak and wine-soaked to do any good. It was nothing but release. I guess I was born with a big appetite or maybe the appetite was a substitute for something else. My people were rigid and not very affectionate."

Shayne rolled over on her stomach and looked at Miss Phoney through somber, thoughtful eyes. "I think you're a very beautiful, very wonderful person."

"Why?"

Shayne shook her head. "I don't know exactly. It's enough, of course, that you were willing to take me in and share what you have with me, but it goes deeper than that. I don't think many people have ever understood you and I think I do."

Miss Phoney's head tilted forward and a waterfall of shimmering hair poured over her shoulders and covered her cheeks. Hot tears poured from her eyes, dripping onto the fine skin of her breasts and trickling downward like gems glittering in the sun.

Night had fallen. Charles and Dr. Carmicheal, after a bountiful supper of crayfish bisque, rice and a green salad were well fed and content. They were seated in the screened front porch of the camp. Dr. Carmicheal smoked his pipe in silence and Charles toyed absently with a cigarette.

The doctor knocked the dottle from his pipe. "Listen to those 'skeeters out there."

Charles nodded. "Good thing this porch is screened." He sighed and stretched. "Boy, what a place to relax. I don't feel like I'll ever tighten up again."

Dr. Carmicheal cut a look at him. "When'll you be a courting Miss Falcon again?"

"I'll take a run in tomorrow and talk to her. Think she'll marry me?"

"I doubt it, but if I were you, I'd give it a little time."

"Time is what I gave the other one," replied Charles bitterly, "and look what happened to it."

"When I said time," snorted the doctor, "I implied that a little inner searching, thought, cogitation, and a few other vaunted human, intellectual qualities be utilized. It is painfully apparent that they weren't used on your previous voyage on the sea of matrimony. Your Angel may be just that but I submit that at the moment you're not quite qualified to judge. It might be a good idea to have some conversation with Dr. Falcon. He's her uncle, as you may remember."

As if in answer to his suggestion, a *pirogue* grated against the barge and the puckish face of Dr. Falcon swam into the light. "Evening," he said brightly. "Could a retired but still occasionally useful M.D. be stood to a drink?"

"Come in, come in," said Dr. Carmicheal heartily. "You can have as many as you can paddle off with."

The spry little man came in and was introduced to Charles.

"I want to thank you for what you did for me, sir. It seems I was in luck all around."

Dr. Falcon, dressed in faded khakis, sat in a rocker with a thump and slid a soft, white hand over his dark hair.

"Lucky was right, but I didn't do anything. Danny and Henry pulled you out and all I did was look things over and give you a shot. Hear you fellows might be my neighbors for a spell."

"That's right," said Dr. Carmicheal. "I'm seriously thinking of taking root here. This lad finally got the good sense to chuck the money marts and live for a while. I'm going to stick around and sort of watch over him. He still ain't dry behind the ears yet. By the way, he's somewhat taken by your niece."

"Angelique? Oh... yeah. Ange is quite a gal, all right." He darted a keen glance at Charles. "Just how taken, son?"

"By all the tests I can devise, I'm in love with her."

"He wouldn't know a test from a tick right now," said Dr. Carmicheal. "He's had one date with her. He was struck blind."

Dr. Falcon lighted a thin cheroot. "Sumpn was mentioned about a drink."

Dr. Carmicheal jumped up and fixed one in a hurry. "Sorry. Glad you reminded me. Think I'll join you. What about you, Charles?"

"No thanks, I think I'll stay sober so I can order my thoughts."

"Not a bad idea," said Dr. Falcon. "I've had mine jumpin' for so long I can do it drunk or sober." He puffed on the cheroot for a moment. "There are a few things about Angelique you should know, Charley. In the first place she's my niece and I think the wide, wide world of her. On the other hand..." He sighed and looked directly into Charles' eyes. "Son, you're not the first man who went off the deep end for her. Ange doesn't mean to hurt anyone. She's a good child, she's lovely and she's a good nurse. However, I suspect a personality disturbance is affecting her. She has had some bumps and she's given some. She talks to me freely because we always have been very close. At the moment, there is a man in her life and she was in a very bad state of indecision.'

Charles sat up. "Did you say was?"

Dr. Falcon nodded slowly. "I hope you don't take this too hard. Angelique ..." He looked at his watch. "She's being married right now."

The explosive silence that followed this announcement was painful to all present.

Finally Dr. Falcon said gently, "That's why I came by. She wanted me to tell you."

"What did she say?" asked Charles in a strangled voice.

"She said to tell you that you're the second best thing that ever happened to her. It seems that the man she's marrying was a backward sort, ill at ease, and unable to play any sort of game at love. He was open and above board with everything because it was the only way he knew. I rather suspect that she couldn't bring herself to believe that he was serious, that he was what he seemed." He paused for a moment. "I hope you will understand, son, when I say she told me all. You proved something else to her. You proved she could be successful as a wife, something I think she doubted due to some unpleasant experience in her past. In essence, that one night with you answered a lot of questions for her. It helped her make up her mind and she had lived for months in torture because she felt what she had for this man was love but she was not sure. You cleared it all up. I'm sorry I had to be the one to tell you."

Charles got up and walking back into the big room, built himself a highball of herculean proportions and came back. "Thanks for telling me, Doctor. I guess I'll live. I ought to be a whiz at cards because I sure can't seem to mesh gears with women."

Danny Pelichet shot the *pirogue* through the water of the South Ramah pit like an arrow. His broad back was corded with muscle and his big arms whipped the paddle back and forth with a monotonous rhythm and made the light craft almost skate on top of the water.

Uncle Henry came to the door of his camp and looked out just as Danny backed water to keep from shooting the bow of his craft into the raft.

Uncle Henry looked at the sweat-soaked shirt and massaged his gums together. "Look like you found sumpn out."

"I did," said Danny shortly as he got out of the *pirogue*. "She never killed nobody. She shook him up pretty rough and she near 'bout clawed the other man's face off, but there ain't been no charges filed and don't too many people even know about it. The judge knew because seems there was some argument about what oughta be done, and I think when Judge Cross got done with her step-daddy, he could see that if he did bring charges she might bring a few herself and then the fertilizer would sure hit the flyin' jenny."

Uncle Henry frowned heavily. "Well, now that's a shame the way they done her but I'm sure glad it ain't as bad as she thought. You gonna take a run up to Tweed's Pass and give her the word?"

"Yes sir, and when I get back I'm gonna hitch that floater boat onto that car and pull it out."

"Reckon it ain't ruint?"

"It won't never be the same again maybe, but it'll be worth gettin' outa the water."

"Why don't you take Mr. Charles with you and show him how to ride a *pirogue?*"

"I done paddled enough for one day. I'm gonna borry Dr. Falcon's motor and hitch it onto that metal *bateau*. I'll take Mr. Charles, all right, cause I got a idea battin' round in the back of my head."

"Like what?"

Danny grinned. "That'd be tattlin'. It'll come out if it works."

To Charles, the proposed trip up King's Ditch to Briscoe Bayou thence to Tweed's Pass was not attractive. Neither was sitting in the deadly quiet of the camp. Dr. Carmicheal, feeling that he would rather be alone with his thoughts, had gone to bed. Dr. Falcon after he had finished his drink left for his own camp.

Charles nodded numbly, "Sure, Danny. I'll go."

The metal boat with Dr. Falcon's motor affixed to the stem muttered slowly up the swift current of King's Ditch, Danny's headlight spraying out through the jungle, then up ahead glittering from the ripples of the swift current. Charles sat hunched in the bow, his breast a heaving turmoil of sick pain. First, his wife ... No, there was no comparison. In her case there had been vows exchanged. Edna owed him nothing. She had her own life to live and if anything she had given him a boost when he was in sore need of one. Charles shook himself angrily. Why was he trying to blame the women in his life for what had happened? His wife, maybe, should bear some blame but neither Angelique nor Edna should be censured. They had given themselves to him freely, joyfully. He had taken and lived in the sharp, perfumed air of delirious ecstasy. That had been his reward. Should he demand more? Could he demand more? Charles began to feel better. Introspection had never been his long suit and now that he had indulged it gave him a sense of relief, of confidence. Danny cut the motor and tilted it out of the water.

"Gettin' too shallow for the motor," he said and took out a paddle, stroking rhythmically along.

"Don't you have another one?"

"No sir. You just set comfortable up there. I'll take care of the paddlin'."

Danny looked at the dejected slump to Charles' shoulders and pondered for a moment. Something had happened, he was sure because where Charles had been alert and affable when they first met, he was glassy eyed and silent now.

"Sumpn worryin' you, Mr. Charles?"

Charles chuckled without mirth. "Plenty, Danny. What would you do if a woman you loved married another man?"

Danny thought for a while. "Well, now, looks to me like as many times as that's happened there must be sumpn that comes to your rescue. There ain't no good way for me to tell you what I'd do because there's some difference in me 'n you."

"Difference...like how?"

"Well, white folks look like they lets these sorta things get under their skin more than colored people do. Now if that gal was the last one around, then I might get up a head of steam myself but there ain't no shortage of women...I mean top-notch women. Cream-of-the-crop women. Sumpn in your voice makes me think maybe this ain't the first time it happened."

"You're right. It's the second time it happened."

"How'd you feel about the first one?"

Charles saw where he was being led but he couldn't veer from the path now and be truthful. "Pretty much like I did about the last one, I reckon."

Danny laughed softly. "Looks like number three is just around the bend."

"Out here in the swamp?"

"Well, I was just usin' a figger of speech, but there's a lotta things in this swamp I ain't ever seen. It could be. Guess I can jerk this motor off again. Water's deeper now." He pointed to another stream that joined King's ditch. It was wide and somber as the headlight revealed it studded with gaunt stumps, relics of long dead cypress giants. On either bank, gum trees festooned with Spanish moss whispered back and forth like old men sighing over past glories. Banks of water hyacinths rustled quietly and gave off a faint perfume. "That's Number Four Road...just for general information."

"Why do they call these streams roads?"

"Well, they was cut out, cleared and used as float roads bringin' logs outa the swamp."

The motor coughed into life and the boat nosed up the ditch picking up speed as it went. They reached Briscoe Bayou, turned left muttered slowly south, nosing in and out between stumps and logs that spotted the bayou. Sometime later Danny's headlight picked out another wide stream that opened off Briscoe. Into this he turned the boat, throttled the motor back to bare steerage and in a few minutes eased it up to a dock that was secured to a big log raft. Charles could see that there was a shack situated in the middle of the raft and through the rickety door he could see beams of yellow light creeping through. Danny threw the motor hard to starboard and forced the stem around until the boat was sideways to the raft. He caught a rafting spike and held the boat steady. The door opened and Miss Phoney stepped out ... oblivious that her cheap cotton dress admitted the light behind her and silhouetted her lavish figure in considerable detail. Charles drew in his breath sharply.

"Evenin', Miss Phoney."

"Evenin', Danny. What are you doin' way up here? Runnin' your lines?"

"No'm. I'd like to have a few words with Miss Shayne if I could."

"Sure! Honey, Danny's here to say something to you."

Charles, still admiring Miss Phoney's plenteous charms, was so unprepared for Shayne that he nearly toppled from the boat. The light shone on her fine hair so that is seemed her face was circled with a halo. He swallowed, a sudden dryness in his throat. Never in all his life had he ever seen such a perfect picture of the multiple distillation of everything that was attractive in a woman. Her curves fairly took his breath, a veritable Diana, tall, strong, her head held high with regal calm ... almost with arrogance. She was dressed in faded khaki shorts and some sort of shirt that had been bleached by sun and washing with the tail tied close beneath the surging elegance of her firm, high pointing breasts.

She came to the edge of the raft and fell with feral grace to one knee. She crossed her arms on the other. "What is it, Danny? Bad news, I suppose, or you wouldn't have come all this way."

Charles stared at her open-mouthed, unbelieving fearful that it was all some sort of phantom conjured up by the drink he had taken.

Danny palmed his headlight so it would cast a light but not glare directly in her eyes. "No'm.... contrary wise, I guess it's the best news you ever listened to. The man ain't dead. He's some used up, but he ain't dead."

For a long moment, Charles watched her face as immobile as a block of oak, but so heartbreakingly lovely that a sick, stifling ache began to rage in his breast. While he watched and devoured the pristine purity of her features, he noticed the sensitive nostrils pinch and flare, twitch once more, then a flood of tears poured from her eyes and down her cheeks to splash on the shoddy material of her shirt. Her lips moved woodenly.

"*Thank* you, Danny... *Thank* you more than you'll ever know. Thank you even more for coming all the way up here to tell me. God... I have so much to thank you for."

Danny was decidedly uncomfortable. He turned a dusky red and shifted his position on the boat seat. "I didn't believe it," he said quietly. "Then when Papa said he just knew it'd all come out all right, I had to know. I know Judge Cross, so I called him up and hinted around till I got him to tell me the story. He wanted to know if you were all right. I told him you was fine."

"I'll never forget..."

"Er... This here is Mr. Charles," said Danny hastily. "Mr. Charles Carraway. He's a camp neighbor and I brung him along for company. Now I reckon we better be gettin' back..."

Shayne gave Charles a perfunctory nod. "Thanks again..."

"Maybe," said Charles, desperately striving to prolong the interview, "she'd like to go back with us." Vaguely he understood that she had been in some trouble involving possible murder and had been running from the consequences. Oddly, it seemed to attract rather than repel him.

"We'd be glad to take you out front, Miss Shayne," assisted Danny.

Shayne stood and looked into the calm grey depths of Miss Phoney's eyes. She could read nothing there but she sensed the loneliness, the poverty of her life now that Fletch was dead.

Shayne faced Danny again. "No... not tonight. Sometime maybe I'll come out... Right now I'm in no hurry."

"Yes'm... I reckon maybe Mr. Charles will take you back to town whenever you want to go."

"Of course," said Charles with alacrity. "Any time at all."

"Thank you," replied Shayne without looking at him.

"Me'n pap'll pull your car out tomorrow," promised Danny. "I'll take the pan off and let it dry out good. The pit ain't muddy and maybe it didn't take too much damage."

Danny yanked the outboard into life and they pulled away from the raft and headed for Briscoe Bayou. Charles was acutely annoyed at the departure. He had to stifle the impulse to leap overboard and swim back. For what? The girl had been barely civil to him... and was he indeed so fickle that every pretty face he saw would mean the upset he had suffered twice in his short sojourn in Louisiana? Charles wallowed in misery and self-pity. What sort of man was he anyhow? On the same night that the news of Ange's marriage crushed him flat, he had met another girl who had so shattered him that he felt disembodied, scattered, emotionally dismembered. He carried the image of her, the way she fell to her knees on the raft, the ineffable grace of every move she made, the exorbitant purity of every line of her body, the somnolent fire of her green eyes, the delicacy of her features that lost no strength to delicacy, the exquisite mobility of her patrician nose and the melting tremulousness of her full, passionate lips... passionate lips. Charles tasted the phrase in his mind and felt so disconsolate that his throat became thick and interfered with his breathing. That she had hardly looked at him ... that the darkness had prevented her getting a good look at him, none of these obvious things seemed to ease the aching conviction that she had rebuffed him with finality. Past Number Four Road, Danny cut the motor for the shallow water and let the boat drift with the current.

"Right likely lookin' lady, wouldn't you say?"

Charles shrugged listlessly. "She never even looked at me ... Who is she, Danny?"

Danny told him the story, as much of it as he knew. "You know," he continued, "sometimes you just knows quality when you see it. I ain't never seen her dressed up but she's one of them women who don't have to. You feels it like Papa knows when sumpn's gonna happen." Danny cocked a bright brown eye to the misery reflected on the back of Charles' head. "You had one misery comin' and another'n goin'. Look like you is a regular playground for the miseries."

"Something," averred Charles with conviction, "is dead wrong with me. Three girls and all of them flatten me for the count. Looks like I don't know my own mind."

"Was they all sumpn like Miss Shayne?"

Well, that's hard to say. That's another of my failings. The newest one is always the most beautiful.

"I guess that's one of Nature's savin' ways. Looks to me like you got a mind what knows its way around even if *you* don't know it. Remember me sayin that the world is full of high-class gals? Looks like you run into one ever time you turn around." Danny laughed softly. "And that ain't near 'bout bad, the way I looks at it. Looks like you're more like me that I thought ... and more than you had any idea."

Charles sat straighter. The way Danny put it, things were going about normal. He respected the big man's opinions because they seemed to spring from the very bosom of rationality. He went straight to the essentials whereas Charles was prone to deviousness, thereby losing himself in the mire of circuitous thought. Edna had rejected him out of hand. Angelique had been confused and their association had been a dose of calomel for her emotional liver ... had purged her of doubts and delivered her into another man's arms. Shayne ... he tasted the name over and over. What an odd name! How well fitted to her as a person. She had ignored him with a completeness that sent him deeper into the glooms from which he managed to emerge through some hard thinking. What had he expected? In the dark ... rather the half light of Danny's muted headlight ... the first time she had ever seen him. Did he expect her to react as he had?

CHAPTER FOURTEEN

S hayne fell backwards on her bunk and relaxed. She was free.
The law was not searching for her and her job still awaited her
back in Baton Rouge … at the thought, her muscles contracted
hard. Marvin and Archibald were still living in *her* house. That'd
be the first thing she'd do. She'd evict them forthwith if it took
the sheriff to accomplish it.

She felt Miss Phoney's eyes on her so she met them. "Honey,
why didn't you go back with Danny?"

Shayne thought for a while. "I'm not sure, Phoney, except
that I've enjoyed it here. I'm in no hurry to go back. When I do,
I'm putting them out of my house."

"Why ain't you in a hurry to go home?"

"I'm just thinking about it. I can get a job any time. I'm
relaxed out here. I love it. I like your company and on top of it all,
you've been wonderful to me."

"You know I wouldn't want you to stay out here just to keep
me company. Child, you got a life to live. Me … I'm thirty-five
years old. Half of mine is gone."

"How will you live, Phoney … ? And I hope I'll look half as
good as you when I'm your age."

"Live … ?" Miss Phoney stretched like a lioness, nude and
glimmering in the yellow light. "Oh, I guess I'll find me a man
someplace."

"Not the kind you deserve," Shayne sat up. Come home
with me."

"Oh, shucks, kid," said Miss Phoney, absurdly delighted. "You wouldn't want an old bitch like me around. You'd be ashamed of me."

"I don't believe you're a bitch and I think you'd act within the limitations of good taste. I certainly wouldn't try to dictate your morals."

"I'm as immoral as a bitch coon," said Miss Phoney, apparently reveling in the fact. "But you're right. I'd be a lady in your house."

"The reason why I want you to come and live with me is because I like you and I think you deserve to be exposed to some good men."

"Hell, I'd probably lay them all over the place and they'd soon see what a free livin', free givin' trollop I was. They wouldn't respect me."

Shayne laughed and lay back on her bunk. "Out of all the men you'd attract ... and maybe lay, as you put it, there'd be one and maybe more who'd marry you just to be sure of a repeat and to cut the others out. Think about it and in the meantime I'm in no hurry to leave."

Shayne, feeling the heat, got up, strolled out on the raft and dived into the cool bayou. For ten minutes she lazed about in the water.

For a while she floated and looked at the brilliant blue vault overhead, the millions of stars and their earthly counterparts, the fireflies that floated close overhead. A bull frog thundered briefly in the swamp and in the distance she thought she heard the gusty bellow of a bull alligator. A water snake, intent on prey, slithered across her stomach, making her start, then smile. She had never been greatly afraid of snakes and now she was afraid of nothing.

Her body, however, knew it deep seated hunger for love. The intimacy of the water caressed her familiarly and made a shudder of reaction flit over her.

She recalled the quiet man who had come with Danny and ran a strip of film through her mind, reliving the scene. He had not penetrated the fog of utter relief that had suffused her when she heard the good news. Now that she remembered, she could examine the details of him. He was rather tall, she thought, his hair dark and well suited to his shapely head... Was it curly, straight...? She couldn't remember. His face had been nice, with a straight, well-shaped nose, his chin rather square and dented, his cheek bones higher than usual and the planes and angles sharply defined.

The look in his eyes filtered through to consciousness and a thoughtful frown creased her eyebrows. She swam slowly back to the raft and pulled herself out to become a fabulous brooch festooned with a million brilliants as starlight caught and danced upon the droplets that collected on her velvety hide.

She had seen the same look in Judge Cross' eyes. A look of undiluted admiration, unmixed with suggestiveness. Desire, *yes,* but not the sort that always made her want to hide or pull down her skirt. It was an honest appreciation for the things with which she was so well endowed and since it came from a man it was impossible to divorce it from desire. He was probably rather nice. She slapped at a familiar mosquito, got up and slipped into the shack, refreshed and relaxed.

Dr. Carmicheal was slightly drunk. "This." he said with gigantic restraint, "seems to be where I came in."

Charles massaged a lean cheek and gusted a tremendous sigh from his chest. It didn't improve things noticeably. "I know how it must sound because I've been all over it myself. There just isn't any way to tell you what she looked like in the half light, dropped to one knee. She was a light in a thin shell of pearl. She was a golden ghost... except that she was too solid and strong. She was a gem in a nest of dark satin..."

"Jumping jehosophat and General Jackson," snorted the doctor. "Did you speak to her?"

Charles pondered for a moment. "I don't remember that I did. I may have, but I..."

"Be quiet and fix yourself a drink. Fix me one while you're at it. Your maundering. Imagine being in the presence of a vision like this and not remembering whether or not you spoke to her."

Charles fixed a drink for himself, a powerful one and one for the doctor...not so strong.

Dr. Carmicheal accepted his drink with entirely too much flourish.

"How does it happen that you discover this and manage to look so dodrotted unhappy about it?"

"It doesn't present an attractive picture...falling like a ton of bricks in minutes...seconds, maybe, for every pretty face you see. What sort of creature am I?"

"A creature favored by the gods...you sniveling jerk. You've seen three that sent you like that. Hell, in my time, by the time I was your age, I'd bumped into a hundred."

"Yes, but you didn't fall in love with all of them."

"That's what *you* think. I do it even now. I just got over the dreadful malaise with which it infects extreme youth. It's a wonderful experience...repeatedly." The doctor softened visibly, "Son, couldn't it be just coincidence that you've run into three really topping women? Couldn't it be that you might go forty years without meeting another...perish the thought."

Charles took a mighty draught and sat down. "It could be. You sound like Danny. He thought I was crazy deploring the incidence of high-class women."

"Danny's right because he has never tried to diddle with his subconscious. He's on speaking terms with it. Better do some serious thinking on the matter."

"I'm not impressed with my ability to do serious thinking."

"Me neither," agreed the doctor cruelly.

"Honey?"

Shayne started and looked up. She had been staring at a small, slender gar and the gar, equally interested, had been staring back. As Shayne started, the gar disappeared with a whirl of its tail.

"Yes."

Miss Phoney sat beside her. They were both dressed in ragged shorts and faded men's shirts with the tails tied beneath their breasts. "Honey, this ain't no good for you."

"You mean staying in the swamp?"

"Yes. You got money, you got a home, you got friends and people you oughta be with."

"What have you got, Phoney?"

"Me..." Her big silken-skinned shoulders shrugged tiredly. "Well... *hell*, honey, all I got is a face and a tail... but..."

"But nothing. I'm not going to leave you down here to rot."

Miss Phoney's big grey eyes dampened. "That's sweet of you but you don't want me hangin' around..."

"I've got to go back to Baton Rouge" mused Shayne, half to herself. "I'm going to run them out of my house." She sighed. "But it won't be the same." She looked forward the top of the towering cypress snag that time, lightning, storm and flood had not been able to kill. "See that snag? It's a friend of mine. I was just talking..." She chuckled. "Not talking, really, but almost... to that little gar when you called me. He's a friend of mine. Danny's a friend of mine. Uncle Henry's a friend of mine. You're a friend of mine. Probably the best producing friend I ever had. In town I have just one friend. Judge Cross." She hugged her knees and rested her chin on them. "He'd love it down here."

Miss Phoney sighed. "Looks like you got a skudge of friends in the swamp."

"Yes, I have. You know, I'd like to see that man who was with Danny last night."

"Sort of had a notion to see him myself... Not like you, of course. That boy's class, a mile deep. Danny didn't tell us much about him, did he?"

"No. I'd rather find out for myself. I have the strangest notion about him."

"I got a fair to middlin' feelin' about you'n him myself. Le's go visitin'."

The *pirogue* shot through the mouth of King's Ditch like a bolt from a crossbow carried by the racing current and almost ran down a head that projected from the surface of the water.

Miss Phoney backed water with a sudden surge of her long paddle and the bow missed the head by inches.

"What the hell are you doin' stickin' your head up right inter my boat?" she flared with savage impatience.

"What the hell do you mean shooting at me with that hod blasted scow?" roared Dr. Carmicheal who was taking his morning constitutional. "I'll have the law on you."

"How'd you like the flat of this here paddle alongside your head?" yelled Miss Phoney in reply.

Dr. Carmicheal grinned engagingly. " You must be Miss Phoney... and you, my dear, could only be the wonderous Shayne."

Shayne laughed. "I'm Shayne Bennett. This is Mrs. Euphonia Unger. We're not so wonderous. Are you naked?"

"I am that and if you two will just ape on across the pit and chat with Henry for a moment, I'll pull out all covered with shame and receive you at yon camp and feed you a breakfast like you've never et in your life."

"You ain't such a stinkin' ole cooter after all," averred Miss Phoney generously.

"Thank you, my voluptuous amazon. I'd like to view you from a more advantageous angle."

Miss Phoney looked at him with interest. That might not be a bad idea," she said engagingly and showed him a mouthful of hard, white biting teeth. "We'll be back soon as we load up with the grub Henry bought for us."

The breakfast was as advertised, consisting of mounds of fluffy, buttery scrambled eggs, hot biscuits, country smoked ham, grape jam, and coffee. Charles, who had finally tom himself from the sack, after a dunking in the chill waters of the pit felt rather more like a human being. He ate gingerly as though not certain whether the food would stay down. Also he kept his eyes on Shayne until at last the others ceased conversation and watched him. He came to with a snap and blushed furiously.

"Sorry," he muttered and bent his head to the food again.

"Now that's what I call a compliment," said Miss Phoney with a smile that managed to be maternal.

Shayne, feeling that anything she might say could deepen his already painful embarrassment, waited until he looked up and smiled at him. Charles wanted to clutch the pain it put in his throat. It was a petal-soft activation of her lips and her eyes were like an ocean tide, deep, sea-green, and so utterly without guile or mystery that he was reminded of Edna. She, too, had not known what it was to dissimulate, to fence, to avoid open contact with situations.

"Y'all go on out on the front porch" said Miss Phoney proprietorially as she dropped a glance at Dr. Carmicheal that almost made him spill his coffee. "Me'n Grampaw got some talkin' to do."

"I resent that," he puffed, but Miss Phoney smiled so brilliantly that he forgave her. When she stroked his thigh with a moist, warm palm he forgot.

Shayne got up and went out on the porch and Dr. Carmicheal devoured the wonders of Miss Phoney's structural divinity with the eye of a connoisseur. "Damn if I ever saw so much, so well placed," he said at length. If he had thought to make her uncomfortable, he was disappointed. She merely smiled again and the doctor felt slightly boiled.

"There's sure plenty of me."

"What is it we have to discuss?"

She poured a third cup of fragrant black coffee and added sugar. "Them two out there."

"What about them?"

"I think it would be a good idea if they got together." She regarded him warmly. "Since I sorta think *we* will."

"We *will?*" His voice broke like a callow youth's. He cleared his throat and strove to order his thoughts. Miss Phoney had set in motion a certain endocrine activity that the doctor had allowed to retreat into slothful ways. Rather than merely sliding along the highways of his veins, it was a frothing cataract, a storm of heated reaction. "Well, now..."

"I think they're just right for each other..." She got up. "I'm tryin' sumpn. You mind?"

"Me..." His laugh was a crazy cackle. "Hell no. I don't seem to have a lot to do with *any* of this."

She closed a large, bright eye, owlishly and stroked his weathered cheek. "Just keep that in mind."

He sighed and watched her undulating body float to the porch door. It seemed boneless, as flexible as rubber but strong and so healthily abounding with energy and somnolent lechery that the doctor felt faintly inadequate for the first time in his long, active life. Every move she made in some way managed to make a flat announcement to all who saw that here was a woman, passionate and ready for the things which nature had so plentifully endowed her.

"Honey," she said with a lowering wink that Charles didn't catch. "Why don't y'all take the vittles on back to the shack and put 'em up. I see Danny's got the car pulled out and dryin'. Maybe y'all'd like to ride inter town this evenin'. I'm gonna stay here and he'p Grampaw clean the camp."

Shayne stood up and impulsively gave him her hand. He took it because there was not much else he could do.

"What sort of a *piroguer* are you?"

"Er ... probably not too good."

He wasn't and only the girl's certain balance and sure hand with the paddle, saved them. Placed as are all *pirogue* passengers who are not expected to do much paddling, in the bow, Charles was in for an hour and a half of as torturing a ride as he could ever remember. She remained in his mind's eye as he paddled awkwardly along as he had seen her last, holding the boat steady for him, her face calm, her lips mobile, damp and as lush as ripe berries, untinted by cosmetics, her body fabulously poised without consciousness, without effort. He could see the shadow of fine long muscle that flickered occasionally beneath the milk chocolate creaminess of her tanned skin. Even as they rode he could feel the balancing effort of her softly, rounded buttocks as they corrected every off move of the frail craft and he could sense the motion of her strong arms and the sure thrust of the paddle. She was wearing white shorts and a sleeveless tan cotton shirt that was stretched to the bursting in the front.

He sneaked a backward glance and she flashed him a quick smile. "Tired?"

"No ... not really. I've got to get used to paddling, I suppose."

He hoped he had not shown the shock she had given him. Everything his mind had been telling him had been true but it fell short of complete truth. Her long legs had been stretched somewhat, braced against a crossmember, the cuffs of her shorts open a little, revealing a suggestion of faintly tinted underthing so full of firm, fine flesh that it was stretched to nothingness. Charles swallowed jerkily and missed a stroke, sending up a shower of water.

"Just ship your paddle for a while," she said sympathetically. " I'll shoot her along."

"Not tired," he said. 'Just clumsy."

She regarded him with frank appraisal and compared him to Marvin.

Marvin was undistinguished. Charles was diametrically opposite. His shoulders were improbably broad, his waist thin and his head had the set of a man accustomed to deci-sion, leadership. His face was rather reposed and his eyes full of vague pain, but these things in no way rendered Charles ordinary. In fact, they in some manner set him further apart. Marvin...

A sudden lascivious charge of retrospective reaction lashed through her and reached Charles through the timbers of the *pirogue.*

He turned, saw her face and eyes, saw the depths of emotion that had her in its grip, wondered urgently for a second, then averted his gaze, feeling as he did that he had intruded, that he had taken a peek behind a very private curtain. Had he known, he would have been shaken to his core because she hadn't seen him glance at her, still in the thrall of the memory of Marvin's rabid embrace, the shrieking of her nerves that followed his searching hands, the leaping transient fear when she knew that there could be no resistance, dissolving her last fluttering effort of token resistance.

Another shudder racked her frame as memory throbbed her through the doorway of her first taste of woman accepting man utterly, completely, finally. A sob jerked her body and made Charles turn around again.

"Shayne... is there something...? I..."

"Nothing, Charles," she rapped out, crashing out of the rev-erie, angry at herself, annoyed that he had been a witness to what seemed an unavoidable re-living of something that had been momentarily, infinitely precious to her, only to see the raving animal burst out in Marvin and shatter the fragile petals of the flower of first love, trample them and beat her with the savagery of an ape-man.

She became nauseated and rested her paddle for a moment, the current starting the bow around. Charles dug in his paddle and tried to keep the bow straight, but it came on and only a quick effort by the girl saved them from possible capsizing.

They reached the shack finally and Shayne held the stem against the raft while Charles got out gingerly. After they stowed the food, there was a moment of embarrassment for which neither of them could have accounted.

Shayne broke the silence. She touched him gently on the arm. "Do you like the sun?"

Her body went taut when she realized the real reason for asking him. He was *man* and she was *woman*... woman that had been thwarted after being aroused to the pinnacle of woman's attainment, whose body had fretted and smoldered and resented its fetters ever since. Woman whose magic, unseen tentacles of demand were subconsciously reaching now for man, wanting him, desiring him with nothing so complicated as the kind of love of which men write in verse and novel, but with a love that is as organic and all being as thirst for water, hunger for food, protection for an infant and need for warmth in the presence of cold.

"Sun...?" He blinked stupidly, his reception quivering from the might of her broadcast... knowing and yet not knowing... knowing but unbelieving... frightened with the freezing fear of some unknown cataclysm... something he knew to be of unearthly wonder... fear because of that knowledge... fear that such ecstasy would be unbearable, that in the red pall of paralytic joy some awful power would make a plaything of him. "Sun... sure I like it." As a matter of fact he had been something of a sun worshipper during the war whenever the press of service didn't bind too severely.

She turned and took out the old quilt and walking past him, she spread it on the raft.

Slowly, with that innate grace which she displayed without knowing that she did, she sat upon it, unbuttoned the cotton shirt until there were but two buttons holding it together over the leaping insurgence of her breasts, then sank back and stretched her legs out.

She placed her palms beneath her head and closed her eyes and sighed deeply.

Charles gazed at her for a moment feeling that he had suddenly been mortally injured.

She lay on the quilt very still for a moment, then her body twisted into a graceful serpentine curl and relaxed...relaxed muscularly but deep inside she was in torment because she could feel the glazed incredulous regard that flowed from his eyes like a stream of radioactive rays.

She could feel the tumult inside him that matched her own and though the sun beat down fiercely it seemed only to add to the heat of her racing bloodstream.

He rubbed his hands against his shorts and felt the moisture of his palms as they skidded past the garment onto his thighs. He examined the round, full-fleshed contours of her thighs, to the magnificently turned symmetry of her lower legs, the almost microscopic deposit of hair that was copper gold in the sun, the shaded rises of her breasts that punched the cloth of her shirt up and glowed softly under their canopy of protection.

Charles went weak and sank to his knees. He stretched out beside her as taut as a bowstring, not feeling the sun but receiving the riotous broadcast of attraction he had never know before.

He turned his head and watched the slightly rounded plane of her stomach with the delightful flower directly in the middle, the symbol telling that she had been born of woman, the rich reward of living which she could in turn bestow upon some child that would be planted within her body drawn into fruition by nature's most irresistible power.

He watched with fascination as her skin began to produce tiny mounds of sweat that grew beneath his eyes until they reached enough volume to flow into streams. Some coursed down her satiny flanks, some rolled into and filled the depression of her navel.

Unable to stand any more in inaction, he rolled toward her and raised himself on an elbow. For a long moment he gazed at the calm, controlled features of her face, watched the infinitesimal nervous twitches that activated the sculptured purity of her lips … neck … cheeks … Once her nostrils compressed faintly then flared and sank back into repose. Then the big eyes opened saw-toothed by the shadows cast by the sun shining through her thick lashes.

Charles felt himself drawn into their depths … A Circle beckoning him on into the toiling surf that would engulf and destroy him.

"Charles …"

"Shayne …"

Two words … words that were sounds of endurance past belief … past their strength. Her body twisted like an eel and leaped to meet the embrace she could see and sense, their lips met, recoiled from the shock, then came together again, ravening wild with the restraint that had kept them apart too long.

The first kiss was one of wanting, drawn into being by the chemistry of nature … man-woman. Positive and negative … negative and positive. She was a serpent in agony and her strength both amazed and dismayed him … details that struck through the mad fog of wonder that smothered them … faint details that were to be recalled later.

"Please don't beat me."

Charles started and staggered under the shock of that poignant cry. Gone was the magic of the moment, the delirious, ecstatic knowledge of what was to come.

"My god, Shayne … *beat you?*"

She strained against his arms for a moment, seizing the unconscious fear that had driven her for a second, realizing in the shocked, frozen face before her what had happened, then she collapsed and wept with a peculiar quiet intensity that ripped him with a pain he could scarcely stand.

He held her close caressing her back, the soft masses of her hair, her shoulders pleading in choked, strangled accents for her to understand that never, never, never could he hurt her, not even a little.

The storm wore itself out from its very intensity and left them feeling whipped and spent. She sat up and wiped the tears from her eyes with the childish employment of her wrists, took in a stuttering breath, then went back into his embrace again, holding him with a need and despair that he could feel and understand without understanding.

"I'll have to tell you... I'll have to let you see why I might say something... like that, again. Please listen, Charles, and don't hate me when I tell you because I've got to tell you ..."

She cried again but this time it was quieter and seemed to measure the relief she had achieved. She told her story, punctuated by moments of tears, of shuddering disgust, of taut bodied hatred and wild resistance. She drew him a picture of the sordid assaults upon her body that had been taken into a situation past resistance ... and when she finished his chest was a bed of raging ache and his own eyes dripped tears of bitter fury.

It appalled him to think that a man, made in the form of other men who could think and reason, could mistreat a person whose wonder and beauty and appeal stalled his senses and tied his tongue.

The sun poured down and sweat drenched them, flowing into the points of contact of their bodies, but it made Charles feel elemental and uncaring ... it was something from her, a priceless excrescence that was an unguent of surpassing sweetness.

He kissed her neck and tasted the salt on his lips and reveled in it. It bore the faintest perfume as though she had eaten nothing but flowers and her body had distilled out their fragrance and sent it through her pores.

"Charles... Charles... *Charles* . ." A deep grateful sob wracked her frame and she clung closer.

His heart hammered at the cage of his ribs with mad cadence flooding his veins with pounding surges of blood. The magic had returned and with it a desire that made any previous experience pale. This time there was no doubt in his mind. With Edna and with Angelique there had been a reticence, a suspicion that he was performing ignobly. He did not feel that way now. Later he wondered about it and couldn't remember that the thought had even crossed his mind.

Without speaking, they rose to their feet and Charles noticed that her shirt had come unbuttoned. He wore none himself and when she caught him to her convulsively he knew then that the shirt had come open and their sharp tipped bulk had made electric contact... while the warm dampness of her lips drove his mind into a whirl...

Again without speaking but with perfect understanding they turned and still half embraced walked toward the little shack.

She released him as they entered, closed the door and turned back, her eyes glowing in the semi-darkness. Lances of sunlight found cracks in the mean hovel ad spotted the floor with little splashes of gold. Slowly, without shame, without coquetry, Shayne stripped off the shirt and let it fall with a hiss to the floor. The shorts followed and now her fabulous middle was obscured by only a breathless splash of skin-fitting nylon. Through it shone the tan-pink advertisement of her healthy skin.

Finally there was nothing and she stood before him like a shaft of Elgin marble... and all he could do was stare and suffer.

With a sob she came to him and for a long time they remained in close embrace, each sensing the other in exquisite detail.

The shack was hot and sweat came from their skin in rivulets but neither was aware of it. Achievement brought a shrill gasp from her throat, then a little gurgling song that was ragged and soft but somehow wedded to the marvelous rhythm that never had a beginning and would never have an ending.

To Charles it was a period of stupendous emotional impact, of moments of raging quiescence...moments of hard chronic hysteria...moments of ineffable tenderness...her eyes would fill and her lips would caress his face and toy with his mouth...not kissing but starved mouthing like a friendly, hungry puppy. Storms rose and shattered them into the rosy twilight of past ecstasy, then begin to mutter and return with increasing force until again they burst over their heads, thundered and beat at them...a sound of hysterical weeping...a sound of the aging but still strong bunk...and at long last, silence

Miss Phoney lay beside Dr. Carmicheal replete, at peace and infected with a strange quiet.

Dr. Carmicheal stared at the ceiling and breathed, "Doggonit."

She raised up and lowered herself until her magnificent breasts caressed his chest. "Why did you say that?"

"Because...I was thinking that why did I have to wait until I had one foot in the grave and the other on a squashed peach before I met you?"

She fell back and pushed a strong arm beneath his head and brought him to her. The heat of her powerful body seemed to sear him. Their mouths mingled and Dr. Carmicheal became a man that surprised even himself. Later she lay flat and stared at the ceiling. She was so quiet that he turned his head to look at her. Twin rivulets of tears were trickling from her eyes and into her ears. Her hair lay in heavy disordered waves, glowing dully. Dr. Carmicheal felt choked up and there arose a feeling for her to which he had often advertised himself superior.

"Why are you crying, Phoney?"

"I don't think I know," she said with a ragged sigh. "Maybe it's because you're the first man who ever made such beautiful love to me before stretching me out. It wasn't just that to you. It was more...much more. I've been handled too much not to know..." She sat up and taking his hand slid it down her flank to a thick, satin-skinned thigh. "It was almost like you was in love with me…" She turned her head. "Not that you could ever be in love with a bitch like me."

He reached up and pulled her down, kissing her with such finesse that she writhed like a snake. He palmed her temples and pushed her head back. "Suppose I told you that I might just be in love with you?"

Her eyes were steady and soft. "I don't think you'd tell me you were if it wasn't so."

"I salute your perception. I certainly wouldn't." He kissed her again. "Phoney," he said so softly that tears started into her eyes again. "You've made an old man very happy."

"You ain't all *that* old," she assured him stoutly, "and you're the first man who ever treated me like I might be sumpn … sumpn else than a lay job … you kinda treated me like a lady."

Miss Phoney and Dr. Carmicheal were seated on the porch drinking tall highballs when Charles and Shayne shot out of King's ditch and angled over toward the camp.

For some reason unknown to him Charles was roaring with laughter and Shayne was shaking her paddle at him.

"As Henry would say," said Dr. Carmicheal, getting to his feet, "I'll be a suck egg crawfish. I *never* heard the boy laugh like that."

"Maybe," said Miss Phoney comfortably, "you'n him's *both* got sumpn to laugh over."

He grinned. "Honey, you can sure say that again."

Shayne dropped the paddle to Charles' seat and thrust it forward, pinching him painfully. He jumped, lost his balance and fell with a splash into the pit. Shayne shrieked with glee and paddled swiftly away, leaving him floundering in her wake. She paddled to the camp with him still trying to catch her but she outdistanced him and climbed out on the barge weak with laughter.

Across the pit Uncle Henry nudged Danny and grinned. "Things is lookin' up."

Danny chuckled. "Remember, I tole you the other day I was gonna try sumpn. Looks like I succeeded pretty good."

"Reckon her car's gonna be all right?"

"It's dryin' out right good. In a few days if it don't rain she can drive it away."

Uncle Henry lit his pipe and puffed for a few minutes. "Well, looks like we got us some good neighbors."

"That's right," agreed Danny. "I'm gonna make a hunter and fisherman outa Mr. Charles."

Uncle Henry nodded, then frowned. "Looks like a man like him'd bust loose some time. Looks like he too easy goin'."

"Can't tell about them quiet types."

"That's right. I've knowed a few that was tigers when the time come.'"

"Maybe Mr. Charles is one of them."

"Could be. He got the build for it. Then there's them two men ..."

"What two?"

"Miss Shayne's stepdaddy and other one she messed up ... I'm gettin' me a feelin' ... ticklin' my stump, sorta."

Danny cut the old man a glance. When he got a premonition that tickled his stump, things were sure to happen. "Uh oh," muttered Danny with a shiver.

Uncle Henry nodded. "Yep. It's one of them kind. Now I got to wait around till I find out what it's all about."

CHAPTER FIFTEEN

In the midst of an excited atmosphere of high altitude happiness, problems poked their ugly heads around the corner. Shayne and Charles had been taken to the vicinity of Patty-U Bend by Danny to be initiated into the mysteries of fishing, Pelichet style. Miss Phoney had taken the *pirogue* to Tweed's Pass to get some clothes suitable for Shayne to wear to Baton Rouge. That left Dr. Carmicheal to sit on the houseboat porch and reflect. He was fifty years old. Miss Phoney was about two thirds that. Moreover, if he was any judge she was a woman with a gigantic appetite for men ... an appetite, that, ancient giant that he had proved himself that day, knew he could not hope to assuage over the long haul. He made a highball and sat sipping it sparingly.

Across the borrow pit Uncle Henry sat cross-legged on his small porch and took in the endless wonders of nature the swamp afforded. He was as placid and patient as a crane waiting for a fish and the fact annoyed Dr. Carmicheal to distraction. Irritably he put down his glass, walked to the screen door and opened it.

"You're a hell of a neighbor," he bellowed ill temperedly.

Uncle Henry, startled from his reverie, almost dropped his pipe. "What I don now?" he inquired mildly.

"You let me set on my butt over here and drink Bradsher's Special Age and don't even offer to come help me drink it up."

Uncle Henry grinned until his gums showed. "Well, now if I'm actin' up like that I better do sumpn about it."

"That's what I been thinkin' for thirty minutes," grumbled the doctor and going back into the big room brought out a fresh bottle of Bradsher's and a glass. By the time he made it back to the porch, Uncle Henry was clambering carefully up on the barge.

Uncle Henry accepted a chair and a drink. "Know what I was thinkin' when you hollered?"

"Nothing good, I'll be bound," grumbled the doctor, frowning.

Uncle Henry chuckled. "Well, now, it wasn' 'specially good or 'specially bad. I was thinkin' that till a few days ago didn't none of us know nobody else among us ... 'cept Miss Phoney, of course ... Now look what I got A new family. Here I is drinkin' with you like we was brung up together. Danny's got Miss Shayne and Mr. Charles and gone with 'em. Danny don't cotton to ever' body but he couldn't rest till he took 'em fishin'. Come fall, he'll have Mr. Charles lopin' all over that swamp night and day and then we'll eat good."

"Eat what?"

"Ever eat any deer meat what hadn't been run to death with dogs? Ever eat wild-duck jambalaya cooked the same day the duck was killed? Ever eat a coon what was killed last night all parboiled with onions and garlic and red pepper then slow baked till he's sorta black brown ..."

"Oh, be quiet. First thing you know I'll be hungry and'll forget my troubles."

Uncle Henry cocked a bright eye at him. "*You* ... got troubles?"

"Yes, me. I reckon I can have troubles if I want 'em."

" 'Course you can ... but most people don't want 'em.

"Well, me neither." Dr. Carmicheal felt really young and for the first time in twenty years, the desire to confide in someone. Then with characteristic forthrightness he did. When he finished, Uncle Henry was silent for a while. He drained his glass and held it out for a refill.

"And don't spill none o' that fine stuff."

He sat back and twisted his drink, deposited it carefully on the floor and sat back, sucking his lips in and compressing them between his gums. He turned and faced the doctor. "What you hopin' for ... me to be some sorta prophet?"

"Hell no. I'm just wondering if I hadn't better take myself on back to the badlands and leave this thing like it is."

"When's the last time sumpn like this hit you?"

The doctor thought for a moment. "There's a small battle about that goin' on in me right now. I keep havin' to choke down the feeling that it never happened like this before."

"When your nature tells you sumpn, you better listen. Now I'm gonna tell you sumpn and since I ain't your nature, you can listen or not, as it might suit you. You got your mind made up that Miss Phoney might be too much for you. I can see that. Well, as she is right now, that might be true. Here's one thing you ain't ever considered I don't think. I ain't one of them brain doctors but I done studied people for a long time. I got a notion that over half the wav she is right now is because she ain't got another thing to interest her and ain't had for many a year. Down here people eats fishes, get drunk and rolls around at night. There ain't anything else to do. 'Magine Miss Phoney in a big fine store with plenty of money to buy herself clothes. A car to ride in, peoples lookin' around at her ... and b'lieve me will look cause she is one fine woman. Them shoddy clothes o' hem can't even hide it. People like the man she lived with, Mr. Flitch Unger, all he was doin' was drinkin' and waitin' to die. He didn't have no future, he didn't have no hope. Since he didn't, she didn't neither. Now that can all be changed. Now she ... if you're the mind to do it for her, she can hold her head up. She can wear good clothes and go to the picture show. She can talk to other wimmen about shoes and stockings and how much lard oughta go inter biscuits. She can tell about that flat she had comin' back from that card party and what sorta coat she's gonna buy come winter." Uncle Henry picked up his drink and leaned forward. "Man, if you can't see what you could mean to Miss Phoney ... If you can't see what a new woman you could make outa her, then I guess maybe you *better* go on back to them badlands."

Dr. Carmicheal sat, partially stunned for a moment. He nodded slowly … as though in a dream. He shifted his weight in his chair. He made the ice tinkle in his drink. "Henry, looks like I had to wait until I was almost too old to learn before I ran into a man who was smart enough to teach me anything."

Uncle Henry chuckled and swallowed the rest of his drink. "Oh shucks, doctor, all I done was part the moss so you could see the game. It ain't always easy to see sumpn like that if it's too close to you."

Dr. Carmicheal sat back and closed his eyes, relaxing completely for a long moment. Henry Pelichet could read and write but he could hardly be called an educated man, yet the doctor doubted if many an educated man with no knowledge whatever of the academic features of psychiatry could have gone so completely to the heart of the matter with such surgical accuracy.

"I knew when I invited you over that I had a better reason than to let you drink up all my good whiskey."

Uncle Henry grinned. "Speakin' of good whiskey … What you savin' it for, hard times?"

Dr. Carmicheal laughed a good deep laugh of release and contentment and reached for the bottle. In the distance he heard the hum of an outboard motor and he saw them returning. All was well.

As they rode toward Baton Rouge, Charles drove slowly and thought hard. Shayne, slim and delectable in nothing finer than a pair of blue jeans and red cotton shirt, huddled against the door and apparently thought just as hard. Her hair was pulled tightly back exposing her face that in its calm repose was beautiful past anything Charles had ever seen. A glance at it set his heart to aching fiercely. At length he spoke.

"Shayne, we've just got to talk about us."

She looked at him and in the dark her eyes seemed abnormally large. The lights from a passing car made them gleam momentarily like an animal's.

"I've been thinking about that, Charles. Let's don't." Charles, who had been treated to the same dose twice before, felt that dying at the moment would be a pleasure. Of one thing he was mortally certain. If Shayne refused him, then he didn't care about anything. Nothing mattered and he might as well be dead.

"Look," he said desperately, "I love you. I haven't known what it was. I just thought I did. I want to marry you. I want it to be soon. That's what we've got to talk about. I have to know or ... " He shrugged helplessly.

She slid over and threw an arm lightly about his shoulders, resting her head on his shoulder.

"I'm very sorry, Charles," she said contritely. "I shouldn't have said it that way. I was afraid you weren't sure. I *am* sure. I love you like I love my life but things happened so fast.<a> I thought maybe we should wait ... I wasn't sure about you."

He brought the car to a panic stop. "Then ..." He seized her face in his hands and brought his own close. "Then you *will* marry me?"

"Yes, Charles ... even if it has been too quick ... Oh, Charles, yes I'll marry you and the sooner the better."

Their embrace was one of a mélange of mutual fears, hopes and prayers. It was one of two people wanting each other with a fierce desperation, fearful that as in the past some hurt, some obstacle would interfere.

He released her suddenly. "You don't know how sudden I can be," he said with a laugh that broke and scattered like shattered glass. As soon as he reached Port Allen he called Dan Woodward who, luckily, was in and poured a story of such desperate urgency into the man's ears that he agreed to perform the miracle and go with them to get an emergency license which would stretch to the limit every political string Dan could pull.

But it was done and in less than two hours Mr. and Mrs. Charles Corbett Carraway, the Third, walked away from Judge Cross' house. The two older men stood on the broad veranda and watched them out of sight.

"Dan, I met that girl a few years ago and ever since that day I've cussed the generation I was born in."

Dan Woodward, tall, thin and tanned, grinned and hunched bony shoulders. "I thought you got all fired interested in a hurry when I called you. I doubt seriously if Toby Schmidt would have come down and got that license for me."

"He'd get it for me," said the judge smugly. "I read his mail."

They pulled the car into the driveway and Shayne started to get out. Charles put out a hand. "When we started this, I decided to let you carry the ball and I'd sit in the car and wait. As it is, you're my wife and I'll go in with you."

She pressed his hand and her eyes brimmed with but I'll be glad to have you along."

Marvin and Archibald Denny sat in the living room as though it were their own. Marvin was drinking and from the looks of Archibald he had been touching the bottle, too. Marvin was still bandaged as the terrible nail slashes had become infected and for a few days it appeared that he might lose his eye that she had slashed so badly. It was still bandaged. They started as Charles came in behind Shayne. For a moment there was a battle of gazes, then Shayne said, "I offer this not as an introduction because I'm not concerned with him knowing you as people. This is my husband, Charles Carraway, the Third, of Carraway Chemicals. Charles, Marvin and Archibald Denny."

A heavy, thick silence fell and during it Marvin and Archibald turned red. Then Archibald showed that he had been drinking indeed. A sneer lifted his upper lip.

"It is too bad that I cannot with conscience congratulate you, Mr. Carraway. In fact, I feel sorry for you. Sooner would I mate with ..."

He stopped because a hard hand had fastened itself in his shirt front and twisted it so cruelly that his face began to purple. "You're an old man," grated Charles, whose veins were raging with berserker blood for the first time in his life. "I'd hate to spread you all over that wall but I didn't come here for your cheap congratulations." He shoved Archibald violently into the chair. "Shayne and I came to tell you and ... *this*," he indicated Marvin with a toss of his head," ... to get out of this house. You have until tomorrow night."

Marvin was not quite sane. Never very stable and now warped completely out of reason by what Shayne had done to him, distorted and accented by her treatment of him as a school boy, his desire for her, his more recent injuries, and continuous drinking, lost every vestige of human control.

He leaped to his feet and swung a smashing blow at Shayne which might have broken her jaw had not an instantaneous reflex imposed a lifted shoulder between her face and his fist. It glanced from the shoulder and struck her high on the head, knocking her sprawling.

Then Marvin swarmed Charles like a madman. Charles, too blind with fury to be surprised, went back a few steps, then dug a vicious right to Marvin's heart.

Marvin grunted and fell back but still had strength enough to launch a kick that caught Charles in the stomach, knocking the wind from him and depositing him on the floor hard.

Archibald leaped to his feet and lashed out with a foot that grazed Charles' head.

Charles caught the foot as it was returning and jerked Archibald into a sliding heap six feet away.

Then Marvin dived on Charles and his fingers seeking and finding his throat.

Archibald got up and prepared to kick Charles in the head again but thinking that Shayne was out of it, had forgotten her. She had shaken the cobwebs from her head and gotten to her feet while Archiblad, watching his chance, was making sure that this time would end the fight.

Shayne, clenching both hands over her head, brought them down with every ounce of power in her body and smashed Archibald in the soft spot just over his right kidney. The man jackknifed backward and screamed like a scalded pig. Down he went, frothing, and his eyes glazed with shock.

On the floor, Charles, whose arms gave him considerable reach over Marvin, was taking a choking that could undo him but at the same time he was methodically beating Marvin's unprotected face to shreds.

Marvin tried to protect himself with his shoulders but finally a sizzling right smacked him squarely over the injured eye and he rolled off sobbing with pain and frustration.

His breath coming in wheezing gasps, Charles stumbled to his feet and backing Marvin to the wall, strove might and main to tear him apart with tremendous short-armed jolts to the midsection, smashing the bloody face when Marvin bent over.

No single blow ended the fight. Marvin just went out on his feet and when the attack slowed sank to the carpet spreading a froth of blood.

For a long minute Charles watched them ... Archibald writhing in agony, Marvin dripping silently on the carpet.

"Let's get out of here," he grated hoarsely. "We're overdue on a honeymoon."

He helped her into the car, handling the door with unnecessary vigor, causing her to flash him a glance.

"Sorry," he muttered, "but for the first time in my life I've smashed a man flat with my fists. I beat him to a pulp and left him bleeding on the floor. He looked at his big hands and long slim fingers. "I smashed him with these. I can do it … just like other hairy-chested men."

"You were wonderful," she cooed, touching a bruised cheek with a hand as soft as the touch of divinity.

Then he remembered. "Damn … but you were getting pretty hot yourself. He knocked you flat and then … I don't know what you did to the old man but you left him kicking."

"I slammed him over the kidney," she said with satisfaction. "I enjoyed mine as much as you did yours."

He chuckled. "Together we make a mean pair. People had better leave us be."

Uncle Henry lay on his bunk and scratched his stump reflectively. "Now that do beat all," he remarked almost to himself.

"What does?" Danny wanted to know as he shoveled down the last of a big soup place of rice, white beans and pork sausages.

"This here stump. About five minutes ago it was tryin' to jump plumb off. Now it's quiet as a mice."

'Nerves quit jumpin'," diagnosed Danny.

Wasn't no nerves. This here stump is my prophecyin' leg. 'Member the other day I said it was sorta twitterin'?"

"Yeah. I remember that all right. What you prophecyin' right now?"

"That's the trouble with it. I knows it's happenin' but I got to wait to see what."

An hour later Charles and Shayne walked down the levee to the camp and gave a hail. Uncle Henry pulled a spread over him and answered. Danny threw open the door.

"It's Mr. Charles and Miss Shayne," he said to his father. "Y'all make it all right?"

"Better than that," said Charles in a new voice. "Meet Mrs. Charles Corbett Carraway, the Third."

Danny yelped with pleased laughter. "Well what you know 'bout that?"

"Didn't waste no time, did you?" sang out Uncle Henry. "Y'all come on in and le's drink a toast. I'm in my sleepin' clothes but I'm covered. Danny, get out that Bradsher's."

They filled glasses and allowed Uncle Henry to propose the toast. He raised his glass and eyed it critically. "Here's to my people. They'll always be my people because we sees with the same eyes."

"Amen," said Charles profoundly and Shayne's eyes grew damp.

Uncle Henry put his glass down. "Looks like you been in a scuffle."

"I have," said Charles with savage satisfaction. "I beat a man ... I really tore him up ... with these." He held up his cut and bloody hands.

Uncle Henry looked significantly at Danny who shrugged and made a sign to signify that as of now he gave up.

"Better get them hands soaked down good in hot salts water," advised Uncle Henry.

"I will. Is the doctor in the camp?"

"Nup, him and Miss Phoney went back in the swamp to her place."

Charles frowned slightly. "I wonder when they'll be back?"

"Well ... er, I don't think I'd 'spect them back any time tonight."

Charles was so thunderstruck that Shayne let go a burst of silvery laughter. "You didn't know?"

"No, I certainly didn't."

"Things, when they happen around here," said Uncle Henry, "got a way of happenin' fast."

"Will you cross us, Danny?" asked Charles.

"Yes, sir. Right now."

The camp was theirs and the night was theirs and no one intruded on either. They showered together and their bodies touched and leaped in tremendous response. She hugged him tightly. "I notice a difference," she said, her lashes stuck together with soft rainwater, shading eyes that were limpid with love.

His hand stroked the length of her long smooth back, causing her to Shudder and grip him tighter.

"What's different?"

"Me ... us. We're here, we belong to each other. There's plenty of time. Yesterday there was some sort of frantic urgency something that drove us along headlong grasping madly for what we wanted ... as though something would snatch it away."

He nodded soberly and kissed her with gentle longing.

"That's what had me just about thrown out last night. I knew I'd die waiting for something ... anything that could assure me you wouldn't get away"

There was another kiss and it lasted longer. Shayne smiled tremulously. "I said there was plenty of time but there isn't *that* much."

"You're so right," he said and picking her up carried her to the bed they had chosen.

"But Charles, I'm still wet."

"Who cares? We'll make the doctor take this one tomorrow night ... We'll take over Miss Phoney's shack for the rest of the honeymoon."

They kissed again ... Her eyes opened, tensed, slitted momentarily, then rolled back in delirious joy and the smile that shone from deep within, witnessed by her lips, was a thing he would long remember. So was the night.

THE END